THE GRIP
OF IT

THE GRIP OF IT

JAC JEMC

FARRAR, STRAUS AND GIROUX   NEW YORK

Farrar, Straus and Giroux
18 West 18th Street, New York 10011

Printed in the United States of America
First edition, 2017

Library of Congress Cataloging-in-Publication Data
Names: Jemc, Jac, 1983– author.
Title: The grip of it / Jac Jemc.
Description: First edition. | New York : Farrar, Straus and Giroux, 2017.
Identifiers: LCCN 2016041347 | ISBN 9780374536916 (paperback) |
    ISBN 9780374716073 (e-book)
Subjects: LCSH: Haunted houses—Fiction. | Psychological fiction. | BISAC:
    FICTION / Literary. | FICTION / Psychological. | FICTION / General. |
    GSAFD: Horror fiction.
Classification: LCC PS3610.E45 G75 2017 | DDC 813/.6—dc23
LC record available at https://lccn.loc.gov/2016041347

Designed by Jo Anne Metsch

Our books may be purchased in bulk for promotional, educational, or business
use. Please contact your local bookseller or the Macmillan Corporate and
Premium Sales Department at 1-800-221-7945, extension 5442, or by e-mail at
MacmillanSpecialMarkets@macmillan.com.

www.fsgbooks.com • www.fsgoriginals.com
www.twitter.com/fsgbooks • www.facebook.com/fsgbooks

1   3   5   7   9   10   8   6   4   2

To Jared,

for your patience, humor, compassion, and grace

410. A person can doubt only if he has learnt certain things; as he can miscalculate only if he has learnt to calculate. In that case it is indeed involuntary.

411. Imagine that a child was quite specially clever, so clever that he could at once be taught the doubtfulness of the existence of all things. So he learns from the beginning: "That is probably a chair." And now how does he learn the question: "Is it also really a chair?"

—LUDWIG WITTGENSTEIN, *Zettel*

THE GRIP OF IT

PROLOGUE

Maybe we move in and we don't hear the intonation for a few days. Maybe we hear it as soon as we unlock the door. Maybe we drag our friends and family into the house and ask them to hear it and they look into the distance and listen as we try to describe it and fail. "You don't hear it? It's like a mouth harp. Deep twang. Like throat singing. Ancient. Glottal. Resonant. Husky and rasping, but underwater." Alone in the house, though, we become less aware of it, like a persistent, dull headache. Deaf to the sound, until the still silence of ownership settles over us. Maybe we decide we will try to like the noise. Maybe we find comfort in it. Maybe an idea insists itself more easily than an action.

Maybe we make eye contact with the elderly neighbor next door. He watches through his window. The moving truck pulls up. We freeze on that odd instant.

Maybe Julie's foot breaks through a plank on the front porch when she steps outside to phone her father to let him know we've arrived safely. Maybe the board breaks months later while we're enjoying the weather with a glass of lemonade. Maybe we fix it right away. Maybe we ignore it for a few months. Maybe we try to convince ourselves that we should get settled before worrying about any repairs. Maybe I make one of the hidden basement rooms into my darkroom. Maybe I start taking photographs of everything: of the stain on the wall and of Julie putting away the mismatched dishes in the cupboard, and of the neighbor emerging onto his front porch and retreating almost immediately.

Maybe the neighborhood children ring the doorbell. Maybe it's some faulty wiring. Maybe that faint chiming is something else entirely—a thing we will only recognize later. Maybe something as simple as a doorbell deserves our dread occasionally. Maybe we're foolish to stay calm for as long as we do.

Maybe I hear a sound and Julie doesn't. Maybe sometimes Julie cocks her ear and says, "What was that?," and I haven't heard a thing. Maybe it's possible to become deaf to something, to block it out. Maybe it's not there for both of us to hear at the same time. Maybe we should remember our fear of the undercurrent when we go to the beach. Maybe we should stay inside and tell each other stories that are further from the truth. Maybe we should share something genuine for once. Stories from the deep, honest pits of us. But what if those buried, fetid stories are the ones that have bubbled to the surface? What if they're right there, balanced on the edge of our teeth, ready to trip into the world without even our permission?

1

THE REAL ESTATE AGENT, with his waxy hair and perma-smile, keeps stopping to listen, waving his hand, saying, "That's just the house settling."

We think the house seems more than settled and wonder why he's calling so much attention to the sound and look at the handsome dark wood trim and how many closets are hidden within closets and we stare out the picture window at the woods butted up against the backyard and we probably wouldn't have heard a thing if he hadn't mentioned it.

But we *do* hear a noise, and now that we're listening, it *is* unsettling how much it sounds like moaning, but not the bellow of someone in pain, more like an incantation, some sort of ritual snarl.

So we look at each bedroom carefully, hoping to be proven wrong about this place, hoping to find something that convinces us the house is not, in fact, exactly what we've been seeking and we ask the agent if we have to worry about crime living so near the woods and he explains that the woods are bounded on the other side by a beach and there is nothing to be afraid of but waves, and we smile politely but, in our minds, we think, *A wave can overwhelm and a wave can take away.*

We snag on that, but the agent barrels forward, hustling us to the unfinished basement and pretending not to hear the sound in an obvious way and he disappears around a corner and we follow him, only to find him gone.

James and I look at each other, concerned, until a section of the wall spins around, and there stands the agent, face plain, matter-of-fact, saying, "Secret compartments. There are several of them in this room alone."

He emerges and squats down, lifting up a three-by-three section of flooring to reveal a small, finished crawl space below us, an empty concrete cube, and he reaches above his head and punches up a drop tile to expose another pocket above, lit well, plaster painted a clean, pale blue, and then I reach high above my head, trying to push against other tiles, but they all stick firmly in place.

"Why?" I ask.

"Well, the previous owner seems to have been a bit of a *homebody*," he says. "We're not sure of the original purpose of the rooms, but they do make for a *ton* of extra storage space."

I squeeze James's hand and he squeezes back because we have this way of feeling the same about the unexpected, and I know, like me, he is excited about the secret passages, this being one of the places where we are seamed together, just one instance where we twist in the same spot, mirroring each other and meshing at once.

A stain stammers on one of the walls, a wet grayish blotch, like new papier-mâché edged in black, and I ask the agent about it, and he says, "Water damage, from a leak at the top of the foundation, but it's been fixed."

Another crush of our hands together, and we wind our way back up the stairs.

The agent asks us what we think and we don't actually need time to decide, but James is doing a great job of remembering my instructions. We will not act too eager. We will hide our excitement until we are alone and can take our time to discuss with reason and measure. "We'll think about it," I say. "But we'll let you know soon. We know how quickly a place like this can disappear."

"Ah, yes. Of course," the agent says. "No rush. You've got my number."

In the car, James says, "I don't think that house is going anywhere. *No rush?* That's unusual in real estate, right? Especially when it's so cheap. People should be crawling all over each other to get this place. I know foreclosures can take some time, but *No rush*? That seemed weird."

"I had the same thought. I say we make an offer right away, but we lowball it."

"You're speaking my language," he says. "*Underestimation* is my middle name."

I tell myself not to discredit my husband's ability to predict the odds, that I'm trusting my own instinct, not his. I tell myself we can win even if he agrees with me.

2

MONTHS BEFORE, Julie and I sat in our apartment in the city. We sprawled on the couch. She rested her feet across my lap. I gripped her bare kneecap. I watched a baseball game with the sound turned off. Julie read. She shifted her leg away and I startled at the reminder that we'd been touching. We fit together effortlessly.

This was true until it wasn't. I had made a series of small mistakes. I insisted that none of it had affected her directly. I had only gambled away the money in my private account. I had not touched our joint nest egg or her personal savings. "It's only a matter of time, though. What if we leave the city?" Julie said. I could feel her desperation in the suggestion. She was willing to try anything. I wondered what I'd done to deserve such devotion. "We could buy a house, get a fresh start. You won't be tempted to visit your old haunts. We'll have some security."

I paused. What I said next was true, but it felt like the farthest I could stretch. "I can imagine that. Let's look into it." I watched a new energy course through her. Julie had not heard *maybe*. She had heard *yes*. She pulled her already-messy blond hair into a loose knot as I'd seen her do so many times before washing the dishes. Julie, with her pragmatism and will, started imagining what she might like to do somewhere else. She had a job title that meant nothing to people outside her office. She worked in product development. She decided what to manu-facture and how quickly. I wrote code for start-ups, but it was sloppy work. I repaired holes in the code with duct tape. They triggered breaks elsewhere in the structure. I gambled with a similar flare. I made outlandish bets. Sometimes I took intentional losses because I got tired of playing. The therapist said I tired out on the anticipation. He said gamblers play until they lose because they want to feel *something*, not necessarily a win.

We talked about the sort of place we'd like to go: another city, another country, somewhere more remote. We didn't want to live in the middle of nowhere, but we could stand a smaller menu of everyday options. We readied ourselves for a place where we'd get to know the business owners and ask about their children. I liked watching the goofy grin stretch her full lips thin and wide, the way her sleepy eyes lifted, when she said, "We can offer our leftovers to the neighbors." I couldn't help but smile back. It was such a silly, simple thing to visualize. "You're okay with a small town?" Julie asked.

I said, "If we check out a town and it feels like it will be an endless trip through airport security, maybe we look somewhere else. They can't all be bad, though." We agreed to stay close enough that we could return to the city whenever we wanted to escape.

"Maybe we shouldn't do it if we're talking about our home as a place to escape *from*," Julie said, screwing her mouth up with worry. I laughed, though. The matter was settled.

Julie hunted for jobs a couple of hours away. She found an opening at a company where an old classmate of hers worked. Julie emailed me opportunities in the same area. I told her I wanted to find a house first. Once we knew where we'd be based, I could focus on where I'd push off to each day. I watched those three little half-moons form between her brows as she clicked from the Help Wanted page to the real estate section.

We find the house quickly. Buy it from the bank. Cheap. I commit myself to finding gainful employment so that we can make the move. We drain the joint account on the down payment. I'll need to pay my half on everything else to be sure we stay above water. In a town this small, only a couple of jobs match my skill set. On my way back to the city from an interview, I stop at our new home. It stands at the end of a cul-de-sac, bordered on the east by the woods. The houses across the street are modest, maybe two or three bedrooms at most, nicely mown lawns. No bikes or scooters left in the driveways. The next-door neighbor's home looms big and Victorian like ours. It needs paint and some woodwork. Ours has been better kept up. The street is quiet, peaceful. I remind myself it is the middle of the day.

I forget and then remember to turn my key the wrong way in the door. The lock has been installed backward. I wonder if this is something I will get used to. Maybe I will become an engaged and invested homeowner. Maybe I'll clean and repair things I've ignored as a renter.

The entryway fits two people at most, with a built-in mirrored hat-and-umbrella stand positioned across from a mirrored closet door. Standing here between the reflections, I watch the small hall extend out in a prism on both sides. I realize Julie had been right. I should have gotten a beard trim and a haircut before the interview. I hope the project manager I'd spoken to didn't think the same.

Beyond the entrance, the living room waits, warm and inviting. I lift a window seat to find nothing at all. I pull at the glass door of one of the library cabinets. It sticks, making a clashing cymbal of sound when it finally budges free.

The living room winds around a wall into what we'll set up as the dining room. Dark wood paneling blends into a heavy-based hutch. We are most excited about all the furniture already built into the walls. It means we won't need to acquire as much to make the transition from our small apartment.

A swinging door opens into the kitchen, filled with ancient yet well-maintained appliances. Julie has already complained that they are bound to cost us a fortune in utility bills.

I head up the stairs. To the right is what will be our bedroom, a guest room, a closet, and the master bath. To the left, more doors: another guest room, another bathroom, the entrance to the attic. I hear a louder humming up here, as if the light were trying hard to reach the hallway. I see a shadow fall through the doorway of one of the guest rooms and feel a surge of fear. I edge toward the room, but find it empty. Relief replaces the dread. *Just a bird flying too close to the house*, I tell myself.

Out the window, I see the next-door neighbor sitting in his living room, framed by his home. The man sits very still. I lean in with worry. In a moment he turns his head. He looks directly at me, as though he feels my stare on him. I give a quick wave and he shifts his gaze away.

I go home. I get the job. We pack up our life.

We carefully unload our car full of breakables alongside the movers strapped with three times as much as we can carry. As we pause between loads to look up at our new home, the neighbor's front door eases open with a stiff, loud scrape. The sound draws Julie's eye. "That's him, huh?" she asks, craning to get a better look.

Julie moves to raise her hand, but the door is already closing. She can have a sweet, useless way about her when she thinks it might serve her. After this failure, she sets back to work, lifting the next bulky box and stepping toward the house carefully, her view obstructed.

We show the movers where to put boxes. We stray from room to room, evaluating our purchase again with our new home-owners' eyes. All of it belongs to us now. I point to the base-ment wall. The stain has pulled itself wider. I ask Julie if she thinks so, too, and immediately regret it. We stare. The spot seems to inhale a little, lungs expanding.

"Could we have thought it seemed smaller because we were so eager? I knew that inspector wasn't very good," she says. Julie places her hand on the discoloration. "It's dry." She leans her face into the wall. "It smells like mold. Chemical, bitter. Do you think a leak might still need fixing?" She pushes her nose around with the back of her hand.

I feign indifference. I want to take back the worry I've caused.

"You're the one who noticed it, but I'll call someone to take a look," she says, already annoyed.

"I can call someone."

"But you won't. It's better if we acknowledge that now." She mashes her nose again, trying to stop the itch.

3

"WHAT'S THE HURRY?" James asks. "We'll be in this house for the rest of our lives."

I prefer to unpack quickly, eager to organize, insistent on accomplishing what I can so I'll be ready for whatever other surprises need addressing. I don't know how to relax with boxes around. My instinct is the opposite of what James suggests: I want to revel in the milestone of homeownership and that requires settling ourselves in. James is sprawled on the couch blocking the entryway, propped on one elbow, flipping through his phone. I gather all the packing paper and shove it into a trash bag. I collapse the boxes, and when the racket of my cleanup ends, the sound of the house reminds me of itself again, that ringing hum. "*What* is that noise?" I ask James.

He raises his head with a question, but sees my frustration and stays cool. "It's the electricity. It's an old house. I said I'll call an electrician."

"You've got your phone right there," I say.

"It's Sunday," he responds.

I turn and catch sight of the neighbor watching from his living room window. I wave, but he doesn't return the gesture or look away. "The neighbor's pretty nosy."

"Yeah." I try to tell if James's *yeah* means that he has also noticed or that he's merely accepting what I've said as true or if the response is automatic, not attentive.

I assess the cluster of pots on the cocktail table. I have no affinity for Pueblo ceramics, but my stepmother, frustrated with my lack of particular-gift requests, decided to turn me into a collector. I appreciate the classy neutrality of the geometrics, but still feel a tilt of resentment at how many of the jars I now possess.

I set a couple on the mantel. I carry two trips' worth to the bookshelves and randomly punctuate the empty space. The remaining pots I leave together on the coffee table, but when I consider the arrangement and count them, the number comes up short. "Huh."

"What's up?" James says without lifting his eyes.

"We're missing a pot." I glance around, counting again.

"Probably got packed in a different box."

"That would be an entirely reasonable theory *if* I didn't remember feeling so proud that I'd fit them all into two perfectly sized boxes."

James rolls his eyes and I know why: because this is precisely a thing that would bring me joy, boring to anyone else, but thrillingly efficient to me. He's about to look back at his phone when his eyes stop in the dining room. "Is that it?" He nods toward the table, and sure enough, there is the missing vase.

"You fink."

James laughs. "I didn't move it."

Could I have set it there and forgotten? Could I have had it in my hand on the way to the kitchen and put it down? This seems like the only answer, so I accept it. "I don't remember doing that at all."

"Ooo, so spooky," James growls because he's sure I must be wrong, that I must have placed it just so, that my habits of organizing and arranging are so second nature, I needn't even think to make them happen, and, really, that's exactly the definition of a habit, right?

"You moved it. I know you did," I say, setting myself on the arm of the couch. I run my hands through his dark hair, longer every day. First it was job searching, then night after night of goodbye drinks with friends, then packing: so many reasons a twenty-minute visit to the barber wasn't possible. I tuck a lock behind his ear and let myself admire the rakish quality he acquires when his hair grows to this length.

"I know, I know. I'll get it cut soon." He doesn't look up.

"It does have its charm when it starts to curl like this." I let my hand wander down to his chin, lifting his face from the screen.

His eyes glint and he sits up. "Oh, it does, does it?"

"It does." I feel my mouth buckle into a grin and keep my eyes trained on his.

"I should make the most of this power before you Delilah me in my sleep." He turns to kneel on the cushion of the couch. "Should I use my magic for good . . . or for evil?" He reaches around to squeeze my hip.

"Good."

"Very well. Maybe a christening of our new home then?"

"A prudent idea." I lean close. "We wouldn't want to risk ending up in limbo."

"Definitely not worth the risk." He closes the distance.

4

ON MY FIRST walk through the woods, I find neighbor kids playing a game called *Murder*. One kid has to hide and think up a way to have been killed. Then, the others have to guess how it happened. I can see only one of the children, hanging over a high branch. I hear the others below trying to determine how the body has gotten into the tree. I try not to get too close, worried I'll interrupt.

I walk through the woods to the beach. I try to place odds on the different ways a dead body would arrive in the branches of a tree. My therapist said I should turn thoughts of gambling, odds, even mathematical ratios, away when they come into my mind. I look instead at the way the private sections of beach form one long, uninterrupted strand, comma'd with rowboats and picnic tables. I unmoor myself and wander back to the house. I look for the children, but they have finished their game.

At the edge of the trees, I am surprised by how far away the house seems. I had remembered the yard as smaller. I trek through the long grass. I find Julie making a salad in the kitchen. "I was thinking about how we found this place. Already I can't remember," I tell her. I kick off my shoes. I rest a hip on the counter beside her.

"Oh, I have the clipping." She sifts through a pile of papers: signed contracts, first utility bills, a bevy of gaudy coupons. "I know it's here somewhere. I kept all of this stuff together. The language was odd, something like *the right house has found you*, and it talked about all the storage, needing updates, nature *nearer by than you could dream*." She pages through again with no luck.

"Not to worry. I was just surprised I'd already forgotten."

Julie gives me a look full of sly skepticism. "James, you wouldn't remember because I was the one doing all of the hunting." She rests her long arms on my shoulders. I feel her wrists cross behind my neck. "But that's the way I wanted it." She kisses me.

I want to argue. I want to say that I remember finding different listings in the real estate sections. My only memories, though, are of her rejecting my suggestions. She covers up her slights with sweetness. I give up. I kiss her back.

5

JAMES AND I met on a blind date when he answered my personal ad—a situation that horrified my friends. I'm not talking about a hygienic online dating website. This was a time when your best bet was to put an ad on Craigslist. My ad was simple, asking if anyone wanted to hang out—an act that, to an outsider, seemed desperate and unsafe and strange.

The flood of responses was to be expected, as any woman willing to post a picture is sure to receive a good many suitors no matter her looks or the content of the ad, and I got satisfaction from the attention, even if most of the responses were from tired creeps and the socially catastrophic.

I met several men for a drink in the following weeks, sometimes three in a night, but there was no pressure to succeed, even when a particular man's powers of persuasion were high. I did a good job of weeding out the weirdos at the email stage, but I kept talking to all of them until they stopped talking to me, except James, who kept calling.

Connie—an old friend, recently minted as coworker—and I catch up on each other's lives over a lunch break down the street from my new office. "But don't you feel like that's settling?" she asks. "Letting the man have all the control over whether or not the relationship continues? Weren't there men you liked more than James?"

"No," I say, full of honesty and endangered pride, "because it worked out perfectly: he's the one I wanted and I was the one he wanted."

"That doesn't sound like the Julie I knew before. You were so precise and rational about everything. I remember a spreadsheet evaluating the boys in the psychology department based on different metrics." She reaches across the tiny table to clear the hair that's fallen over one side of my face and to cup my cheeks. "Hello, Julie? Are you in there?"

I bat her away and she snorts. "I felt like that *was* the way to be sane in a situation like that. Where did those charts get me? Anthony? He was not a prize. People get so carried away. Not to mention, it's only after that dating bender ended that I recognized the pattern, that I understood why it worked. I mean, I was attracted to James from the start. His body was so solid. He was so dusky eyed and unkempt. He had a certain confidence to him, but it wasn't arrogant. There was a silliness about it. So much mischief in him. I think I was looking for someone very different from me and it wasn't worth thinking about rationally, because I'd cut myself off at the knees every time evaluating the ways the men fell short. Maybe it was *me* who stayed tuned in to *him* and so he's the one who ended up sticking around."

"Okay, enough about how much you love your husband."

Connie tries to change the subject, but I pull it back. I want to push her to consider a different way of being. "But I do think there could be multiple soul mates for a person, you know? People are beautiful and complex enough that I believe I could find multiple people in the world to love."

Connie drops her mob of curls into her hand, exasperated. Her whole face opens up. "Really. How can you be married and believe that?"

I swat her hand. "Isn't it more romantic that I *could* be with anyone I want, but it's James I *pick*? Isn't that beautiful?"

"That's not a soul mate, though," she replies.

"Sure it is; I can't imagine life without James, but I *can* imagine life with someone else."

Connie hurries away with the conversation to talk about her half-hearted despair at what she'll wear to an upcoming event—anything to get away from willingly recognizing the limit of her point of view.

I play along. "I swear, that has got to be the one-hundredth stroller that's passed this window in the last hour."

"Welcome to Normal Town." Connie clinks our glasses. "This is really where you want to be?"

"It is!" I don't want to tell her about James's gambling problem. Not yet, at least. I want to believe that we can get past it and start fresh and that it's possible for it not to matter, and so I say some things by way of explanation that aren't *un*true. "I was so into trying new restaurants and scouring event listings for the hottest tickets in the city, but at some point I said to myself, 'If I order one more cocktail named after an old Western, I'll shoot my own horse.'"

Connie laughs and so I name a few. "Lonesome Dove, Purple Sage, Death Comes to the Archbishop. When I saw one called Wounded Knee, I knew we had to get out or else."

Connie's eyes are wide with horror, but she keeps the joke up. "But *you*! You wanted a little piece of that homesteading life for yourself, so you set out for small-town America."

"There *is* a lot more land out here." I shrug.

"But the company is a bit more . . . limited," she says, hinting.

I deliver her the compliment she's asked for. "But who needs variety if a high-quality selection is available? I was ready for a change of company. It's good to get out of your comfort zone. And those people knew *all* of my secrets. Too many ways information could leak out. I was ready to go into hiding."

"I'm happy to be your only security risk." We laugh and another baby rolls by. She points and says, "One hundred and one."

6

I GRAB A beer with my coworker Sam on my way home from work. He's not a friend I would pick on my own. In the economy of work compatriots, though, he will do.

We drive separately to the bar closest to the industrial park that our office hides inside.

"Stellar to have you on board, man. Right after I got hired, they appointed a female CEO and she's hired only women since. I thought I was going to have to file a discrimination suit. Where my bros at, ya know? I mean, the office has some nice scenery now, but I want someone to enjoy it with." He chucks my arm a little too hard. I battle with whether I'll share his worldview with Julie when I get home. Is the commiseration worth turning her against my one friend in this town?

The bar is exactly what I expected. Tin signs and faded motel art cover the faux-wood paneling. A fat folder spilling customer tabs is wedged beside the register. Bottles of liquor aren't lined up neatly on display; they're wedged behind tchotchkes.

A bottle of Wild Turkey peeks out from behind a bas-relief placard showing a lady leaning against a stove with the saying THE KITCHEN IS CLOSED DUE TO ILLNESS. I'M SICK OF COOKING. Peach schnapps rests between a taxidermic fox's legs.

We take turns buying a round each, then Sam says he has to get home to watch the game. I compliment his choice of teams; they're doing well this season and I'd have bet on them if I hadn't promised Julie I'd stop. He high-fives me and punches my arm again. I will myself not to flinch.

Sam checks his reflection in a Bud Light mirror. He pinches his goatee to no noticeable effect and straightens the collar of his polo. "Later, man. Hasta mañana." He heads for the door.

I order one more. The old bartender, who's been silent until now, tells me my face is new. "Where're you from?" he says without much interest. He reaches across the bar to wipe down the area where Sam was sitting. I notice the wrong way the last joints of his fingers bend.

"We're from the city. We moved into the big house at the end of Stillwater."

He looks up sharply. "The end of Stillwater, you say?"

"With the wraparound porch, yeah."

"Well, they've all got wraparound porches over there, so you're not helping me much, but you're saying the last one before the woods, is that right?"

"That's the one." I take a sip. "Why?"

"I know a bit about that house. Do you?"

I pause. "I know I live there. What else is there to know?"

"A family lived in that house for a long time, parents and a handful of kids—little slices of people, they were. Pale. Fuzzy."

"But what about 'em?"

He runs his thumb inside the waistline of his jeans, inching up the flesh of his belly behind his thin T-shirt and then letting it fall. "Well, the boy child was seen so little people wondered if he was real. Shined like a shaded bulb, if you know what I mean. Now the girl, I knew a bit because my buddy dated her back in high school. She had troubles. My friend was never allowed in the house, but he was enamored for a short while until her father told him not to come near her anymore."

I ask the bartender for more pretzels. He refills the bowl with a warning: "Careful, those suckers'll make you thirstier, and then you'll be wobbling your car home like the road is a tightrope."

"No reason to reveal the trade secrets. I'll take a glass of water, too."

The bartender fills a pint glass for me. "Now, the girl had a habit. When they were out, she'd keep scribbling in a notebook or on a napkin or any little scrap of paper she could dig up. My buddy said he didn't even think she knew what she was writing most of the time. She'd fill up a piece of paper and then flip it around, start writing the other way. Layers. He said he'd wonder if she was listening to him when he talked, but she could carry on a full conversation while she wrote. I'd say he was a little relieved when her father forbade him from coming round. He wanted to understand, and he was getting the idea he couldn't."

"So what happened to her?" I catch sight of the clock in the mirror behind the bar. I realize I should get going.

"Oh, she ran away from home not long after that. Her parents died, and then the state tried to track her down but couldn't, so they ended up putting the house on the market."

I ask for my tab. I thank him. "I'll be back in case you think of any more stories."

The bartender looks at me as if I've misunderstood.

I drive on the four-lane highway, until the heavy trees thin and side streets offer themselves. I look for kids running around after dinner. I hunt for the lights of TVs in windows, but still, the neighborhood is silent. *It's later than I think*, I tell myself. *You wanted quiet. This is what you wanted.*

7

JAMES IS LATE getting himself home from work one night, and I consider looking up the location of the nearest OTB parlor, but stop myself. He might still be working or maybe he's made a friend. I wonder why the living room looks so clean and realize James's boxes are gone. The lower shelves of the bookcase are solid now with his collection of crime novels, urban histories, sports biographies. I hunt through the house, wondering what he's done with the rest of his stuff, if he's stashed it in closets. His movies are tucked into the video cabinet. The board games are stacked, haphazardly, in a cupboard in the basement. The desk in the guest room is piled with office supplies. I peek out the back door and find the flattened cardboard boxes slid behind the recycling bin. Granted I've been nagging him to do this for days, but in the end he's finished unpacking before I have. I feel a wave of guilt, and then joy that I won't need to bring it up again, that I can praise him when he arrives home, and then I claim his productivity as my own and give myself the night off from unpacking my lingering boxes.

I wander the yard, surveying what needs to be done. Behind the house, where the birches are dense like teeth in a mouth, I find a spot where the foliage grows weak. A row of stones lines the short end of a patch of dirt. Memorial. What I'm looking at is a grave. I try to talk myself out of it, but I circle the spot, hunting for clues. It doesn't even seem like a secret that's trying to be kept.

A large bird circles overhead, but I know it's my imagination that makes it a vulture, and I look back to our house and then the house next door and see the old man in the window for only a second and I wonder if he knows something about this.

Could there be more of them? I wander, rooting with my eyes, in the backyard first and then through the woods with no luck, and on the other side, where the forest meets the beach, I stop looking down and lift my head to the water, and my windpipe is overwhelmed by a gale, and my breath clogs with the force of it, and my mouth fractures into a grimace as I gasp, and I squeeze the meat of my arms, and I try to harness my heartbeat to calm myself, and my nostrils feel full of sand, and the potential of the moment paralyzes me.

For a second, running into the lake feels like an irreversible decision I should make, but I don't recognize the voice suggesting this, and in this way I haunt myself until I turn back to the house and let my mind peer from above, like a camera strung on a wire, through the branches. Sometimes I am hidden from myself by the foliage, but then I pop into view again, veiled and then revealed until I reach the edge of our yard and stop, still surprised at how close our home is to the woods, dwarfed by the size of it, adjusting to the new scale of the box I contain myself within.

I am feeling unusual, not in a way that I can explain, but preoccupied with the sounds the house is making and unnerved by the space that fills each room and surprised by how quickly I've become accustomed to the wilderness surrounding us, but more than the combination of all of this: I feel like I've turned a full circle inside myself, like I am due to unwind, like I am a spring coiled tight, waiting. I wonder if moving here was a mistake, but then I nudge that idea away and replace it with thoughts of the stress of uprooting our lives, of starting new jobs.

I want to tell James about what I've found—in the yard and in myself—but wonder if I should delay until I know the ending. I dash that thought away quickly, too, wondering why I would want to wait, how I would bear it on my own.

I pinch myself tightly through the back door as if something might sneak in behind me, and there in the kitchen, I kick off my shoes and luxuriate in the way my feet grip the evening-cool tile. I pull open the fridge and let the contents shine on me, warm, like a spotlight.

8

WE EAT DINNER. I tell Julie I've made a friend at work. I keep the details vague. She tells me that Connie just broke up with her boyfriend. She lives on the other side of town, near the high school. Julie's excited to spend more time with her again. The office is fine—nothing special. She can tell the operations manager is going to drive her bananas. When she got home, she says, she took a walk through the woods. She describes a mushroom she saw, and I tell her I'll look it up. I sense a secret in the misses of the conversation. Something hides beneath her skin. Like a mouse running under a fitted sheet. She keeps shifting in her chair and itching.

"Are you okay? You're scratching."

"It must be the dust in here." She eats another bite. I watch her fingernails approach her arm again. She pulls them back. She shakes it off.

I want to ask if she saw the children in the woods. I want to lay out what the bartender told me. We play chicken. We wait for the other to give in and listen.

Julie breaks. "Also . . . ," she says, stalling, "I found a grave." She bites her lip, aware of how paranoid she must sound. "In the yard. It's unmarked."

I don't know what I was expecting, but this wasn't it. Maybe this will serve up an answer for us. I cock my head and I tuck my lips over my teeth. She stands. She takes my hand. We go out the back door. We traipse across the dew-wet lawn. She points at a plot of stale dirt lined on one side with rocks.

"We don't know."

She says, "I do, at least as much as I know anything about this house."

I furrow my brow. All of a sudden it feels as if we're halfway down a dark alley with a stranger who seemed friendly enough back at the street. Julie toes the edge of the plot. In that moment I feel all the love I possibly can for her. I see a wet drop land on the dirt below. I raise her chin to me and have to remind myself not to kiss her when her lips blouse themselves out like that. "Hey, this is nothing. We're having some cold feet, but this is *nothing*. A patch of dirt."

She glances to the house next door. She looks for something, but turns back to search my eyes instead. "What did you have to tell me?"

I hesitate. In this moment of pause, the chirp of the locusts in the trees and the buzzing of the birds in search of one last meal before dark crescendo to a crushing maximum. I think of the hum in the house and wonder if it might be nature we hear. Maybe the threat forms when the sound is filtered through brick and glass. Then the warble dies away. I hear no wildlife at all. The sky has turned a gray blue. The sun is gone. I return to the task at hand. I don't want to upset her even more. I know that I owe it to her to be honest and share my worry, too, though. I tell her about the children in the trees. I tell her how they call to each other. They hunt for a murderer.

Julie acts as if this is less concerning. "That's just kids playing."

I feel hurt for taking her seriously and being dismissed myself. This is how she copes, though. "You're right," I say. I'm proud of her for not taking this trouble on. I try to believe. I think of the bartender's stories and keep them to myself.

9

AT WORK, PEOPLE are polite when they ask about the house and how unpacking is going and I tell myself they don't resent that I was hired as VP of product even though they've all been here longer and know the business better than I do. I tell stories about finding more secret places in the house and about how floorboards shift and we find the blank treasure that is more storage and about how the humidity swells the windows in their frames and how the glass makes the forest waiting behind the house seem wet and close and I say we think our neighbor might be spying on us and they laugh about what they think is my paranoia. I say, "I'll have all of you over soon so you can see for yourselves" and "Fine, don't believe me," and women and men alike huddle at the entrance to my cube to make easy jokes, until the day Connie asks what's on my neck, and I don't know the answer, so she comes over and smoothes the wispy hairs up and tugs my collar down and says, "This bruise. What happened?"

The two of us rush to the bathroom down the hall and I turn my back to the mirror, but also crane my neck to try to see what she's talking about, and when I yank at my collar myself, I realize that the area is tender, but the angle is all wrong, and I can't see. Connie runs to get the compact from her purse, and it takes me a few tries to get the orientation of reflections right, but there it is, a bruise, large and oddly shaped, and we can't see the bottom of it so we shut the bathroom door and lock it and, because Connie is such an old friend with whom I used to change in dance class, and because it doesn't matter, I take my shirt off and the bruise is even larger than we thought, running almost down to my waist. Connie asks what happened and I say, "I don't know," and she gives me that stern look that says both *You can tell me* and *For real? We're going to fall into this cliché?*

I say, "Really, Connie. I'm fucking freaked-out right now," and a million things flash through my mind, but mostly it's those books I read as a preteen: *6 Months to Live, I Want to Live, Too Young to Die.* "Cancer," I say out loud. "It's some sort of blood cancer."

Connie immediately sobers up. "Come on, Julie. Let's not be *dramatic*," and when I look at her with real fear in my eyes, she pulls me to her and she's so bony I don't expect her hug to be as comforting as it is, but I can tell she's watching my back in the mirror, and trying not to grab at the bruise, because she'd seen me flinch when I pulled my shirt off. "Did you get wasted and fall down again?" she asks, smiling into my hair, knowing I've pulled myself together since college, and I can't help but laugh, because even if Connie is not my best friend, it turns out she's exactly who I want in this bathroom with me. She's all

I've got in this tiny new town and she's still hugging me, but I'm trying to break free to put my shirt back on and she won't let go and it's some kind of joke I don't get, and that's why I love her, because she can make me laugh in a nonsense way, and she says, in a spooky voice, "I think it's growing."

I laugh and give her one final push. "So comforting, Con."

She squints her eyes at my reflection, as if she might actually be noticing something, but I pull my shirt down and her eyes snap back to mine, and she says, "Yeah, I'm kidding. Couldn't be."

10

JULIE TAKES HER turn talking to my parents. She puts them on speaker. The picture Julie paints of the house is a bit rosier than the truth. She feels the need to protect us against criticism. It was her idea not to tell my parents about my gambling problem. "They'll offer only worry and help, and we don't need either," she'd said. I felt both better and worse because of this decision. I thought of our vows.

On the call, my mother pipes in with advice and recommendations on what could be done to improve the place, sight unseen. "Have you replaced the hardware in the bathroom and kitchen? That goes a long way. A fresh coat of paint and some new switch plates for the lights. It's those little details that can make a home feel really clean and new." Julie leans her head on the back of the couch, stretching her neck and rolling it along the edge of the upholstery gently. The bruise also goes unmentioned. I turn my finger into a blade and run it across her neck. She lolls her tongue out of her mouth. She knows what she should do to save her own sanity. She waits for my mom to finish so that it's my dad she cuts off.

"Thank you for all of your advice!" Julie's voice is so chipper and believable. "I should probably get to the hardware store before it closes! I hope the two of you have a lovely weekend, though."

My mother responds, "You let us know when you're ready for visitors, okay, Julie? We'll be there in a jiff. Say goodbye to James for us!"

"Will do! Talk to you later!" Julie exaggerates the gesture it takes to end the call. "That they can *be here in a jiff* is not a comfort to me."

I take her hand. "That jiff is longer than it used to be. I'd say you're on the up-and-up here."

She frowns. "Do you want to go to the hardware store?"

"Not really, right?"

Julie sighs. "She has a point. Maybe if we put a little work into the house, it'll start to feel like our own."

Julie, at heart, is a people pleaser, a straight-A student. She's had a series of jobs she hates but can't help being the best at. If someone gives her advice she deems sound, she'll act on it immediately. Julie pulls on sneakers and a jacket. I follow her out and still can't quite remember which way to turn my key in the door to lock it. When I get down to the driveway, she has already installed herself in the passenger seat and put the keys in the ignition for me. "Thanks for driving." It is never something I mind. I watch Julie relax in the seat beside me and we pull away.

We turn onto a side street and then out onto the main road. The farther we get from the lake, the more modest the houses become. Wider spaces separate them. The flat road winds through a tree-lined canopy. Otherwise we'd see all the way to the horizon. When the street spits us out into full light, we pass motels, then condo complexes, town houses, small ranches, and then a section of big old mansions wreathing the center of town. A defunct fountain sits in the middle of a square that's mostly grass with triangular beds of geraniums and lamb's ears. "Could you get any more white-bread?" I ask.

"I'm so glad you care about plants," she says. "I appoint you head of our landscaping."

"If you insist," I say. I think of how I will transform the empty plot of dirt at the back of the yard into a raised vegetable garden. I will ask what Julie wants to eat and grow it for her.

The parking spots in front of the hardware store are full, as are the ones at the pharmacy next to it. "I mean, it's a miracle these places stay in business what with those shopping centers out by the highway. I'm surprised there are this many cars," Julie says.

I pull into a spot around the corner in front of the town hall. "These shops are probably more expensive, too." I let myself out.

"But they're owned by human beings, not corporate giants, and *that's* why we are choosing to shop here." Julie slams her door as punctuation.

Inside, Julie picks the most expensive faucet for the bathroom sink. She chooses the least expensive plates for the light switches, saying, "I can compromise."

We watch as our paint is mixed: Gentle Cream for the bedroom, Mascarpone for the living room, Wind Chime for the kitchen, Croquet for the bathroom.

"Croquet isn't a color," I say.

Julie rolls her eyes.

"Croquet doesn't even tip off what color it might be. Is it green?"

Julie shows me the paint chip. "Gray really, with a greenish tint, I guess."

She lists off items I can grab: a painting tray, rollers, primer, brushes. I gather. I turn the aisle corners expecting to run into another customer, but we're the only ones in the store. "Where do you think all the people are?" I ask Julie.

Julie looks around as if she hadn't realized we were alone.

The girl in the stiff blue apron helping us can't be older than sixteen. When she talks, she hides her braces by cupping a hand over her mouth. I look to Julie because I know this is the sort of thing she'll be charmed by. She is giving the girl a smile I'm sure she thinks is friendly, but it exhibits pained pity instead. "What's fun to do around here?" Julie asks. "It seems like there must be people around. Where are they hanging out?"

The girl looks stunned, as if she's been accused of something. She shakes her head and continues ringing up our items.

A man on the verge of retirement hobbles out of a windowed office to make sure we've found what we need. "Jenny took good care of you?"

Julie is quick with the effusive praise. "Couldn't have been more helpful. You've got a keeper here."

"They all leave me for college eventually. The ones who want to stay aren't the ones I want to keep." The man turns back to his office. "Come back to see us again and we'll keep being here."

"We hope so," Julie says, and looks at me expecting some kind of merit badge. Jenny puts the paint cans in a plastic bag and I ask if she has a box. She disappears into the back to look, returning with one that's twice as big as it needs to be. I accept it and pile the supplies in. We lug everything out to the car.

Julie says, "Oh, an ice cream parlor."

"Let's check it out." I close the trunk.

"Only if you really want to." She keeps her eyes trained on the shop.

"Oh, I *really* want to. If you'd be so kind as to accompany me, that is." I place a hand on the small of her back, a bit damp from exertion, and push her across the street.

In the shop, no one stands behind the counter. We can hear voices through the open back door. We examine the flavors. I know Julie will stick with her standard. Still I ask her.

"Oh, chocolate, of course. You?"

"Maybe eggnog."

"Ugh, James. You don't even like eggnog." She hushes her voice. "And that's probably been sitting in the cooler since Christmas."

"I think it's time to give it another try."

Julie sneers.

I step behind the counter to call out, "Hello? We'd like some ice cream."

"James!" Julie says, embarrassed. "I'm sure they'll be out in a second."

But minutes go by. Still, no one emerges. "Can I go back there now?" I'm not asking permission so much as warning Julie.

"Let's go. We don't need ice cream," she says.

"For real?"

"Yes. It's a sign. No ice cream for us." She pulls open the door. I follow her. As we pass in front of the window, I swear I see someone peek in from the back.

Julie lets herself into the driver's side. She starts the car. I buckle myself in beside her. When we drive past the ice cream shop, I see the CLOSED sign has been flipped. The lights are off. Julie doesn't notice. We reverse our course through the patterns of zoning.

Back under the canopy of the winding road, I ask, "Do you feel better? Having a project to work on now?"

I can tell she feels taken to task. "I know it must seem like I'm throwing money at our problems, but if we think of the house as an investment, this money will all come back to us in time, and if we update little by little, we'll be able to sell the house someday for much more."

"Julie, we just moved in. You're already thinking of when we'll leave?" I have also already wondered about when we might move on, about what might prompt such a decision. Would it be the grave or that noise or old age and an inability to keep up with the demands of a home that size? But thinking about the house as an investment that we'd cash in on is not one of the ways I'd considered it.

She's quiet for a moment. I know our minds pause to shape themselves around that same possibility, of admitting a mistake and moving on, but she spins out of that current. "That's how smart homeowners think, James. I'm an investor, not a gambler."

I tell myself it's not a dig. I tell myself that, if it is a dig, I'm getting off pretty easy.

11

I SIT ON the lawn in the backyard, pulling the thick, multifingered spirals of weeds out with all my might. I thrill when I succeed in uprooting the thick plug of a base from the ground. My back aches and I take a break, staring at that blank spot that hides something I don't want to know. Wide gaps of dirt populate the areas between the patches of grass where the weeds once were. I'll need to add a bag of seed to the list of items to acquire on my next trip into town. I hear what I think is a flock of birds at the forest's edge, but when I look up into the trees, I see a couple of children, arranged high in the branches, and assume there are more I can't see farther in based on the volume of their cries. These must be the children James mentioned. I try to pick out what they're calling to each other, but I can't flip their sounds from chirps to language.

I finger the soil, scraping, unpacking, until it's fresh and loose, and I begin to work my fingers into the earth, get my hands buried deep enough that my wrists feel the cool soil, and let them stay there, feeling fixed in place, grounded, until the chill resolves, and my hands have warmed the earth around them and I feel the dirt go to mud, and it takes a huge effort to pull them up, and the first thing I think when I see them is that these aren't my hands. These are different hands from the ones I dug into the ground. These fingers look longer now and these palms open wider. I stare up at the sun until the light burns my eyes, and I close them, pull my dirty hands to my face to find some darkness. When my sight recovers, and I let the light back in, everything looks clearer. My hands are my own again and I can see veins in my legs that are closer to the surface than they'd been before. The grass looks sharper and the dirt is clumped in pillowy mounds around the holes I'd cleaved and I feel a face right in front of my own, but I am alone, and I know that if I am not alone, it is just some other version of myself that is nearby. I feel breath on my cheeks, and I think of the way my hands seemed wrong, and I inhale and the air is cool and the light darkens and I look for a cloud, but I can't even find the sun because my vision is dark or blocked and I feel a tightness around both wrists, snugger than the dirt had been, but when I pull back, I can move my arms fine, yet the pressure remains. I stumble to stand and lurch-run inside, arms out, muscles taut, the door taking too long to swing shut, and I sit on my wrists on the nice pastel floral couch trying to rid them of that feeling of compression, and my vision comes back in pinpricks as I try to remember how long I'd been outside, try to remember when I'd last eaten. I search for all of my answers in the world, return to look out the back window and memorize the empty garden and close my eyes, trying to imagine I am seeing myself sitting out there, conceiving myself as both inside and outside, and then I feel light-headed and lie down on the living room rug, pace my memory until sleep trips me, and James arrives home, shaking me, sure I've passed out. I wake, confused, and he looks at my hands and ushers me into the kitchen, where he washes them gently with warm water and soap that smells like tea, scrubbing my nails. We are both silent, but his is an assured silence, a silence of faith that says, *Whatever it is, we'll figure it out, but for now I will care for you.* This quiet chimes like a bell, undampered, and I want to thank him for his understanding, for letting this ring, and so I hug him tight, my hands still wet with soap, and I bury my face in the soft flannel of his collar, and he tucks his chin over my shoulder and I feel the scratch of his beard on my neck like Velcro holding us together. He puts me to bed and in the morning I am full of fever, but I pull myself downstairs for water and when I look, there are no longer smudges on the sofa and the holes where I'd buried my hands in the yard have swallowed themselves.

12

AT NIGHT, on the way to the bathroom, I don't turn the hall light on. I trace my hand along the wall. I touch something wet and soft. It reminds me of rotten-apple flesh. I think of Julie's bruise. I run my hand back. I try to find the spot, but I can't. My senses weren't awake. Maybe my fingertips imagined it. I massage my hands with each other to wake them up. At the bathroom, I flip on the light. I can feel my heartbeat in my eyes. My vision pulses slightly. I stare at the tiles behind the toilet while I pee. In the mirror, a darker version of myself follows directly behind me. No matter which way I turn, it's turning immediately before me. I feel a furry smoke spreading its way up my arms. I don't let myself think. I return to our room. Julie shifts when I get back into bed. Shadows caw outside the window. I know what a shadow is.

13

IN TOWN THE checkout lady wants to know my origin. "Where yah comin' from? And what house d'yah live in now?"

Her rangy forearms show threads of muscle as she flips through the book that will deliver her the code to punch in for my peppers and I see her key in the number for jalapeño and tell her, "That's a serrano."

"They're all the same price, ma'am. Don't make no difference." Her eyebrows are drawn on a little too high, and the real ones are starting to sprout below, as if the penciled-in lines were training the hairs to grow in a certain place.

I tell her we moved from the city, and she nods knowingly. "My husband and I bought the house at the end of Stillwater, right before the woods." She glances up quickly, so I ask her, "What?"

She stalls for a moment. "Nothin' at all. That house is fine."

I say, "No, please. Tell me what you know about it."

She eyes me, determining if I mean it, and scans my box of oatmeal. "Lotsa rumors about that house yah might be happier to live without."

"Tell me." I wonder at how she can turn each item without looking so that the bar code will prompt that satisfying beep and watch the ropes in her biceps slacken and strain.

"Woman who lived there didn't leave that house her whole life. Born there and people say died there, too. Nobody ever found a body, though."

"A body?" I say, and I'm not scared. I'm excited.

"That's right. Neighbor said he hadn't seen her for a while. Police paid her a visit, and she wasn't under any rock they turned over. They searched the whole house. They waited. Eventually the house went into foreclosure, then went up for auction. She didn't have any kin or nothin'. House stood empty for a spell, until, well, I guess till you."

"Yeah, the bank told us it had been on the market for a while. We got a great deal." I look down as she settles lemons onto the scale to be weighed. "Who was she? What did she do?"

The cashier limps a bit as she backs up to pull out a small plastic bag for some dripping meat, then resumes her rhythm, turning on her waist's axis the ninety degrees from screen to scanner and back. "Well, her family was real rich, kept to themselves. People talked about writin' on the walls. Messages and drawin's. They painted over it all or replaced the plaster or somethin', I'm sure."

"What kind of drawings?"

"Witchcraft, voodoo, who knows? They say she started young drawin' on the walls. Her parents would holler at her and crash around the house tryin' to get her to stop, but as soon as they calmed down, she'd start up again. Then they gave up, let her go wild. But I betcha haven't seen even a lick of that stuff."

"You're right about that."

"How have yah found the house? Any spooks around?"

I squint. "Spooks? Not that we've seen." Answers can be right there in your ears, unheard.

"People gossip about her still being in there."

I scoff. "How could that be?"

"I agree, bored small-town talk. Flappin' their gums with any rumor they can think up. I don't believe it either. Just givin' yah the full run of the chatter."

I thank her and head out to my car. The hum of the engine sounds almost like the moans we hear in the house, and that has started to become a comfort.

14

JULIE AND I ring the doorbell. Inside, the neighbor plays what sounds like marching-band music, loud even through the heavy brick. We knock on the door and windows. Julie says she can see him sleeping in an armchair. *TA-TA-TAT-TAT.* She has a tray of brownies in one hand. I hold a pitcher of lemonade. Julie says, "How can he sleep through that snare?" We sit on the steps and wait for the record to end. When it quiets, we get up and try again, hammering.

Finally, the door swings open. "Must you?" his voice pounds like a bass drum. We take a step back at the sight of him. Deep creases point like arrows to his bulbous nose. The draw-bridge of his broad lower jaw is pulled up tight. His forehead folds in curtains of displeasure. Extending straight out from the sides of his head, tapering at the ends, his hair, full and white, strikes the silhouette of a tricorn hat, clown hair. He is shorter than either of us, but dense. I am not convinced I could knock him down.

A sprinkler comes on and reaches just far enough to hit Julie. She scurries toward the interior. "May we come in?" I ask. The man takes his time saying yes. We step inside.

His breath strains. He doesn't shut the door. He pauses with his hand on it.

"We're your new neighbors," Julie explains.

"I know that." The man's pronunciation is stiff, each word forced out individually like a finger poked into my chest. A low grumble lines each syllable. I stifle a smile at his gruffness. I think about making an excuse for us to leave. I look to Julie. She is letting her eyes take it all in. She scans casually, but I watch her sight snag on the intricate openmouthed face carved into the newel at the end of the stairs and then on an ancient wooden-box easel jammed beside a plastic basket of rags. She is not ready to give up.

"I'm James and this is Julie. We brought a snack. I hope we're not imposing."

"Then why are you here?"

"Oh, uh . . . to get acquainted," I manage. "It's always nice to know the people living around you, right?"

"I wouldn't know."

"I'm sorry, I didn't catch your name, sir."

"That's because I didn't tell it to you. Rolf! Kinsler!" He barks his name loudly.

Julie says, "It's nice to finally meet you, Mr. Kinsler. Do people around here mostly keep to themselves?" Julie shifts the tray of brownies to her opposite hand and offers one to him.

"I'd invite you to sit down, but you won't be staying long."

Then I smell it. Something fetid and sharp. I look around

the filthy house: newspapers stacked twenty high, mats of fur edging everything. I skim the surface of the room for cats. I know, though, that they can make space for themselves behind and between and below. The air feels coated in a thin layer of grease.

"Would you like to sit out on the porch maybe? It's a beautiful day."

All the lines of Rolf's face scowl themselves more profoundly. "I don't go out much. Eczema, psoriasis, sun poisoning. I'll see you out." He unburdens us of the tray and the pitcher. He sets them on a console table near the door.

Julie looks at me, incredulous. I take the first turn holding out my hand. "A pleasure to meet you, Rolf. We'd love to have you over for dinner sometime. Julie's a great cook."

Rolf grates out a noise that must be as close to a laugh as he is capable of.

"Okay, then," Julie says, glaring. "I hope you enjoy the brownies and lemonade."

We cross to the other side of the threshold. It's possible Rolf exhales "Mhmm" before slamming the door. Halfway across the lawn, we hear the marching-band music again. Blaring horns celebrate our retreat.

"That went well, huh? Anytime we need to borrow a cup of sugar, we know where *not* to go." Julie pulls open our front door and drops herself onto the couch. "I'm going to choose not to take that personally. Is that the right decision?"

I seat myself beside her. "Yes. We tried. No need to push it. Plenty of other people on the street to befriend." I consider whether to speak my next thought aloud and then I do. "And he probably won't be our neighbor for much longer."

"James!" Julie pushes my leg with her palm.

"I'm sure he doesn't leave the house much. It won't be hard to avoid him."

"We didn't even ask him to mind his own business and stop looking at us, though."

"Well, maybe curtains are the next project," I say.

Julie whines, "But I like the light!"

"It's a choice," I say, indifferent to the decision she will make.

She shuts her eyes. "Why must it always be a *choice*?"

"Well, you can always avoid choosing and just let it go."

"*Let it go?* Never heard of it!" Julie's mouth smiles, but her eyes stay shut.

15

JULIE PACKS A bag with towels and bottles of water. I grab my camera. We walk the beach. Julie reads the waves like identifying cloud shapes. She points to a break. I try to see what she sees, but I cannot. We ask each other why Rolf was so resistant to us. We try to reassure ourselves that our visit was normal. Julie says there's a chance we might never get restless here because everything feels so strange. I agree: "I still feel like a guest in our home."

"I just remembered this. Last night in the kitchen, I was having a midnight snack—peanut-butter toast—and I could hear a rustling somewhere nearby, but, you know, the house echoes because there's so much space, and that sound was every-where and I couldn't tell where it was rooted, so I walked around the whole kitchen, wandered into the dining room and the living room, too, and no matter where I went, the sound seemed like it was always above my head, like sand sifting or a plastic bag rustling, but eventually I gave up and returned to bed. I couldn't find it."

"I need to call the electrician. And an exterminator. We'll get to the bottom of it." I say this and then wonder if I want it to be something that easy.

We linger on the topic of the noise. We analyze what would cause this new, more percussive layer on top of the previous drone. We stand at the edge of the waves. We let the sand bury our feet.

We run out of things to tell each other. We share second- and even third-tier stories we'd never bother other people with. Those minutiae calcify into the bones of our intimacy.

Julie's bruise has mostly healed. The purples and browns have faded to a dull yellow that makes me cringe.

Julie turns and sees my face. "The least you could do is pretend to hide it."

I agree with her. Still, it looks as if a part of her were dying.

She insists it was all the moving and cleaning that caused it. "I'm clumsy. And I wasn't eating well for a while there, and lack of iron and knocking myself around with those big boxes—I'm sure that's all it was. I mean, I was so tired I passed out, for goodness' sake." Her eyes flick away from mine. I can tell she doesn't want me to poke holes in these arguments, so I don't. Julie has taken care of herself up until this point. She will take action when she thinks it's necessary. I don't like going to the doctor either. I force myself to detach.

I take photos of the trees and plants, of the birds and squirrels. I pore over the local field guide I'd purchased side by side with the photos and learn our new surroundings.

We talk through what to do about the basement. Should we replace the stained plaster? Paint over it? Finish the basement with carpet and beer signs and a sectional couch? Julie lifts handfuls of sand to rub into her fair legs, massaging them. I set my hat over my eyes to keep the sun away. I lie on my back. I vote for letting it be. "I made that one closet into a darkroom. That's all I cared about really. We have more than our fair share of livable space in that house. Why sink money into fixing up the basement?" Julie doesn't respond. "Do you disagree?" Again silence. I lift the hat from my eyes.

Julie stands many yards down the beach. She seems too far away for as recently as we'd spoken. I get up, awkward in the shifting sand. I walk toward her. "What do you see, Jules?" She is staring out toward the distant edge of the forest, near that rocky point.

"The edge of the inlet there. There's a cave in the rock, up above the water, I think." She turns. "And those kids you were talking about. I hear them now. All the time. I want to know where they live. I never see them with parents, do you?"

I resist the suspicion forming inside her. I know I've caused it. "No, but you were right. They're kids. It's spring. That's where children belong, outside, out of their parents' hair, right? What does it matter?"

"They're creepy, like you said. I thought it was a one-off, a fluke, that they'd get tired of it, but they're always around and it's weirding me out." She walks back to where we'd spread our things. "I'm beat. Let's go make lunch."

I agree. We squeeze through the trees to walk back. We swear we can hear the echoes of the children's voices. Their bodies, though, are nowhere in sight.

16

WE NEVER THINK through why a room ends in one place but the next room doesn't begin there, until one night we awake to our spatial stupidity while I'm washing my face. I find a cupboard behind the medicine cabinet. We find a loose brick in the fireplace and pull it out and stick our arms into the space and can't find a wall within reach of our blind touch. For weeks we assume that a corner that juts into our bedroom is the closet of the room next door, but the next time I'm in the guest room, I notice the closet there is on the opposite side. What inhabits this empty column? I knock, as if that might provide an answer, but hear no echo. I show James, and he shakes his head.

We plant new bushes—boxwood, James's choice—around the perimeter of the property and talk about how there is an earth beneath the earth into which we wedge our spades. At the beach suddenly we are looking for seas beyond the sea.

James says, "Stop. It's extra closets in an old house, fallout shelters and pantries, and we're not used to being prepared."

I say, "I can feel the history in them, though."

At dinner, James lifts his plate to put it in the sink. When he returns to the table, an empty plate remains where he'd been sitting. "It's been there all along," I insist. "I wondered what you were up to."

On walks around the neighborhood I peer into windows, trying to see how our lifestyle compares, and find our same lamp, a bookshelf identical to ours, a TV playing what I know James is watching at home. I walk through our front door and straight out the back and realize it is not our home I've passed through, but Rolf's. I pause at the newly planted hedges and look at one house and then the other and ask myself if what I think just happened really did, but I talk myself out of it. I try to picture my body passing through his house from back to front, like a ghost, but I can't remember any details and so it mustn't have been real, but a daydream on foot. When I secret myself inside my own back door, I find I have to uncurl my fists. Everything I see in our house looks as if it had been replaced with a replica.

17

"DID YOU ACTUALLY go to Rolf's to pick this stuff up?" I set my bag down in the entryway and seek out Julie, who's at the sink washing vegetables.

"Why, hello! I didn't hear you."

"The tray and pitcher on the table. Did you pick those up or did he leave them on the front porch?"

"Neither. I thought maybe you'd gone to ask for them back before you left for work this morning." She shuts off the water and wipes her hands.

I shake my head. She slows, surprise inching onto her face. "Are you kidding?" Her grin wastes. "What does that mean then? That he came *into our home*? Jesus Christ."

I try to think of another way.

"What do we do? Call the police?"

"I'll go over there," I say. "I'll talk to him."

"I'd rather call the police at this point, James. I told you we should have changed the locks. What if the last owners gave him a key?"

"Let's try to keep things civil," I say.

"I'm calling the locksmith. If you're not back in five minutes, 911 is next."

I skip the front pathways and trace a crow's flight across our lawns. I knock loudly, a triple rap, and then a dectet. No one comes to the door. I try the handle. In movies, everyone is always surprised the door is unlocked. I think I'm out of luck. Then, I remember the heavy creak of the hinges when we stopped by. I push harder. The door resists, then opens at once, as if something were slumped against it, but when I step inside, nothing is there.

"Rolf?" I call. Letting myself into his house feels like retribution for his intruding on us. I realize no answer will be provided in this visit, though. The massive portrait above the mantel hitches my vision. A chill runs through me. Maybe it's the sense of being watched. The eyes in the painting track my trespass. A family of four: a father and mother, a young boy and baby daughter. I edge away and my heel strikes something solid. I tumble backward and see it's a pile of old newspapers, toppled now, copies of the same issue. My eyes fumble to focus on the headline. "Kinsler Family Tragedy" repeats itself across a dozen fanned editions. I hear what I believe to be the creak of floorboards upstairs. I struggle to my feet. I shut the door behind me as quietly as possible. The coughs tumble out of me. Once out in the fresh air, I realize how rancid the must had been inside.

18

JAMES HURRIES BACK across the lawn and I catch Rolf in his kitchen window. I flash back to the vision I had of walking through Rolf's house and ask myself if I could have grabbed the pitcher and tray, if I could have carried those things into the house with me and forgotten. I can't talk myself into believing what my mind suggests. I turn away and open the front door. "What did he have to say for himself?"

James looks startled, flustered. "He wasn't home or he was sleeping and didn't answer."

"What do you mean? I saw you go inside and I just saw him in the window. How did you get in?"

"Shit. Then he heard me." James's eyes bug out, the sharp white standing out against the purplish-olive sickles of fatigue beneath. He blinks and the contrast pops again. "The door wasn't locked. I let myself in."

"An eye for an eye, eh?" I try to remember if it was me or James who would have locked our door as we left this morning.

"He'll know I was there. I knocked over some newspapers, too. But get this: 'Kinsler Family Tragedy' was the headline. Multiple copies. Rolf Kinsler. I should have taken one."

"That would have been stealing. We should look that up to see what it's talking about, though."

"They were ancient. Too old to Google," he says.

"Microfiche, then. We'll go to the library."

James is pressing his fist to his brow, hunched over the dining room table.

"James, he came into our house first. He had no right." I say this and trust it. "The locksmith is on his way. You didn't do anything more wrong than what he did. If he's angry, it's what he deserves."

James forces himself to at least appear to agree, and then his eyes focus sharply on me, like something's clicked. "The way he watches us, the fact that he came in without our knowing—something's going on. I'm calling the Realtor to see what he knows. Maybe he can help figure out which of all these stories we're hearing is true. He might know what Rolf's deal is. Do you have the number?"

I'm surprised James wants to act on this right away. Usually he'd put it off and then lose momentum. I pull up the number on my phone and hand it to him and watch him dial. He starts to pace and stops short. "I dialed wrong. It says the number's been disconnected." He dials again and pulls the phone to his ear and then hangs up. "Disconnected."

"How can that be?" I hit DIAL and listen to the same message. "Maybe he got a new number." I pull up the browser to look up his name, but nothing comes up. "What the hell? I must be spelling it wrong or something."

"I am not into this. I'm going to the library this weekend to investigate." For once, I believe James when he says he's going to do something.

I rifle through the papers from the move and search for the Realtor's ad again, but it remains lost.

19

THAT NIGHT, I find a body in the attic and it's hard as diamonds and I look for more. The second body I find is a pile of soft bones and surprising shapes of teeth behind a panel in the basement. In the middle of the kitchen, the third body's nails have screamed themselves out of the retreating fingers of collapsed flesh, a pile of rot that lies there as if it hasn't been moved in decades. I go outside and find a cranium, a tibia, a phalanx, and a pubis scattered from an open grave, as though dropped out of gathering arms, and I assemble them into a skeleton, ablaze under that broad and bleeding moon. I dream these bodies as answers and then wake and stir at how close this nightmare felt to reality. I drift through them again at the breakfast table, these dreams shaped like memory.

I might tell James or I might not. I start to lose track of what I've shared with him and what I've kept to myself. I find myself starting to talk about the sounds in the night, an inconsistency in what the woman at the checkout told me, the new bruise on my hip that's already starting to fade, and then I stop myself: Did I tell him about this already? If not, I worry he'll think I've been keeping secrets. And then, because I don't want to keep secrets, I keep more secrets.

I think James is peculiar for not being more curious, but then I wonder, *What if he's doing the same thing? What if he's hiding his interest and confusion and unease for fear that I'll want to leave? Perhaps he's afraid of returning to the city, to old habits and temptations.* It might be that we're both curious, but we think the other isn't.

If you put your eye to one side of a water glass, you have so many angles to navigate trying to see something on the other side. Four edges of curved glass. Water's opinions: a lens. Most times, your gaze bounces right back to you.

I want time away to see how I feel apart from this place. I want to see what my mind turns up on different terrain.

"James, maybe we should go on vacation."

He tells me he's surprised I would suggest such a thing. "Wait, let me get this straight. Julie—the keeper of the finances, the planner of the futures—wants to go on vacation when we just bought a house? Even I know that's a bad idea."

"Well, we could have done both if we'd made a few different decisions leading up to this."

James looks less angry than discouraged. "You mean that we could do both if *I'd* made different decisions, right?"

I had promised that I would let it go, that I would trust he could change, that it was a quirk, a setback we could get past, that people can fix themselves, that the rest of our lives wouldn't stand the threat of being lost on a missed basket or a worn-out horse. He had promised it wouldn't happen again, but I break *my* promise. "Well, *I* have enough money to do both. I can't help that you traded your future for some dumb wish. That's what a bet is, right? A wish?"

"I thought we weren't going to do that. Is it that bad? Do you want to leave that badly?"

I backpedal, apologize by way of lying, hide my apprehension behind a white flag. "No, you're right. I'm sorry." I finger the rotten yellow spot edging my waistline. I think of the bodies in my dream and keep the deterioration to myself.

We're missing each other.

20

MY TEAM SPENDS a day trying to figure out what's broken with the program we're working on. QA testers run through again and again and can't reproduce the error. "Probably a connection issue then," I say, but the project manager insists it couldn't be.

She tries to explain: "James, we're building this program to teach people customer service. If the program tells the user that a customer asks for a refund and the user chooses to tell her to take her business elsewhere, that should be an immediate fail, game over. Instead, the program delivered a message commending the user on a good choice and promoting them to shift supervisor. Something's broken."

"Customer service isn't really my thing. That's why I went into computers," I joke, but she doesn't laugh.

"Well, fix the computer then," she says, her voice on edge.

Sam offers to lend a hand and finds the mistake right away. "You didn't account for the possibility of someone looping back around to this screen after they'd already succeeded in similar situations." He strokes a few keys. "I'll let Kim know it's fixed."

He walks across the office and rests his arms on the top of her cubicle. Sam leans down and begins talking. When Kim responds, I see Sam shrug. Kim looks back at the programming room, but I turn away quickly.

"No biggie, man," Sam says upon his return. "Even the best of us have to get used to the way content drives the programming."

"It doesn't make sense that someone would make the proper decision once but then make a mistake the second time," I say.

"You're thinking rationally, but not reasonably, man. We need to account for any possible outcome, and the result has to make sense. Sometimes people bomb these things for the fun of seeing how poorly they can do."

I think of every bet I lost. And I think of the bets that followed.

21

JAMES AND I search for distraction. We invite my dad and stepmother for the weekend to show off the house and pick up all that's dropped between us in the hustle of moving. "Where did you get these?" I ask. A small vase of flowers sits in the middle of the dining room table.

"I picked them on my walk through the woods this morning. And then some roses from the bush on the side of the house."

"You can pick the flowers in the woods? You won't get arrested?"

"Of course. This is milkweed and harebell and valerian, I think." He reaches a hand around to pat himself on the back. "*Nice work, James.* I thought it might be a nice touch for Carol. I put a little jar up in the guest room, too."

"I will keep you." His charm can still make me blush.

My parents arrive, and the first thing my stepmother compliments is the flowers.

"That's James's doing. He picked them and arranged them," I say.

"You hear that, Frank?" she says to my father. "James picked flowers! Take a cue. Anyway"—she turns back to me—"I've brought you a housewarming gift that might be a perfect way to showcase James's talents." From the entryway she fetches a gift bag that proclaims CONGRATULATIONS ON YOUR NEW ARRIVAL! beside a pale blue teddy bear. I take the bag from her and raise my eyebrows. "I *know*, but it was the only gift bag I had in the house, and you *have* experienced a new arrival of sorts."

If it were only a case of Carol's being stingy, I wouldn't care, but I know the bag is also a wink that buying a house is the first step toward having a baby, making a *proper* family, a nod to our having told my parents we don't want children. I pull the tissue out and find another piece of Pueblo pottery.

"This one's a canteen!" Carol broadcasts.

I thank her and hand the pot to James. "See if you can fit your flowers into our lovely new vase, please!" James disappears into the kitchen while I show my parents to the guest room.

I make dinner: fried chicken and mashed sweet potatoes and bean casserole—food I know my parents will eat—and James mixes everyone manhattans and my dad drinks too many. He holds forth on whatever he's read about recently and ruffles his wily eyebrows about the injustice of a recently passed law. We perform our incredulity at some new way we're poisoning our bodies and gasp politely at all the random facts he shares.

My dad drains his glass and jingles the shards of ice at James for a refill. We wait for my dad to look away to share a glance. I shrug, resigned that at least he'll probably pass out after the next drink. My dad gets to flipping through the pictures in some history books stacked in the living room. My stepmom retreats into the guest room so she can shower and set her hair in the foam rollers hourglassed with plastic memory.

Alone in our bedroom, I want to decompress and tell James all the things I couldn't say in the company of my parents, but the walls are too thin. Instead, I lie down and close myself around him and hear his breath regularize quickly, but my mind spins. I have trouble getting comfortable and think about how we'll fill the day tomorrow, then, suddenly, right in front of my face, I hear a thick exhale, almost a growl. Hot air through a ragged windpipe; I can feel its moist remainder lingering on my skin.

The electricity of fear almost bolts me upright, but I hold myself down, sure someone is standing right over me. I inhale sharply and try to focus on the darkness. Has some vent above me decided just now to start making this noise? I settle back and attempt to calm myself, beginning to drift off, sure I've dreamed the thing, when I hear it again.

The sound shapes itself, rough and wet before me. I smell the breath, sour and ripe at once. "James?" I whisper.

"Yes." His response is not that of someone half drawn away by sleep.

"Did you hear that?"

"Julie, it was right in front of my face."

"It was in front of *my* face." I find his warm hand under the blanket. We wait for it to happen again, barred from sleep by anticipation, the time fast and slow at once, but neither of us hears it if it does.

I am aching with exhaustion when dawn starts to show through the window and we can finally see that nothing is before us. We drift off and wake late.

At the brunch table, we don't want to alarm my parents, so we keep our secret quiet. My stepmom, her hair already sculpted into a pouf that frames her face like a halo, helps herself to some pancakes and says, "Now, you kids know I don't like to start trouble, but I had such a fright last night." James and I glance at each other, chew slowly. "I was falling asleep, and, I swear, right above me, I heard something breathing, deep and heavy. I thought maybe your father had finally come to bed and was having some kind of attack, but I felt around and said, 'Frank? Is that you?' No response." She pauses. "I lay back down and I heard it again: a loooong snarl. I was spooked. Is that your heating system or something? Do you think an animal could have gotten into those spaces in the walls? Maybe you have an *infestation*?" She whispers the final word, as if the pests might be offended to hear it.

I wait for a moment, trying to decide whether to admit we also heard the noise, but I decide honesty is best. "We heard it, too."

"It was that loud?" My stepmother looks at my dad in shock. He continues shoveling pancakes into his mouth, as if nothing were amiss.

I recognize her misunderstanding as a way out of this exchange, but I clarify, "No, we heard it, too, but it was right above us, right in front of our faces. We could smell it." I wonder what keeps me going, what it is that's encouraging me, if I like seeing Carol horrified.

"Yes!" my stepmother gasps. "That smell was *awful*. I could have thrown up."

Finally, I feel the regret at having been honest release through me like a faucet opening. I stand to reach the coffee carafe, trying to move on.

"This is too much. I'm sorry, Julie. I wasn't going to say anything, but I do not like this house." My stepmother sets down her silverware. She throws her napkin on her plate. "Frank, we're not staying here another minute. Julie, this place is bad news. There's something creepy about it. I couldn't pinpoint it, but, with what happened last night, I know you can do better."

I should have seen this coming. I should have known having my parents here wouldn't help, that my stepmother would be overly critical even if everything went right. I should have protected this space until we were settled and assured and ready to defend it.

My dad says, "I didn't hear anything, Carol."

"That's because you were passed out, drunk as a skunk. You wouldn't have heard a lion roar inside of you. We're going home. I've seen all I need to see. Julie, I'm begging you: get out of here. We'll help you. I'll lend you some money—some money you can keep, but *leave*."

"I think you could be more supportive, *Carol*," I say. She recoils. Calling her by her name instead of *Mom* has been the greatest insult to her since my father married her. "This is our first home. Of course, some things need fixing, but I'm pretty proud of it. I agree it's probably best if you leave."

I can see I've riled her by telling her to go. My father doesn't try to right the situation, only turns his eyes away so it can't seem as if he is taking any particular side.

James and I clean up the table while my parents disappear upstairs. When I hear the front door open, I force myself to follow them out and watch as they load their car, but I can't find any words that strike the right balance of civility and admonishment. I wave as they pull away.

Alone, we examine our bedroom and the guest room for vents and cracks in the window frames. James and I re-create the conditions by lying on the bed side by side. In our bones, we know nothing will happen, and so we use this time to talk, as if we're both trying to convince the other we should stay.

"My stepmother was obviously overreacting."

James takes only a moment to commit. "Absolutely."

"I think the house might lend itself to suspicion what with the secret rooms and whatnot, but really I think we started off on the wrong foot. And I'm certainly not accepting money from her. Even if I paid her back, I'd never hear the end of it."

James agrees, but then he pauses, and I am nervous about what he will say next. "That sound last night, though, that was . . . something alive, right? It sounded like a beast—which, I know, seems crazy—but whatever that was, it wasn't a clog in a vent or the house settling."

I think this is where I might lose him if I agree. "I'm not that certain, I guess," I say, but in my mind it seems clear.

22

I GO TO the library to look for the newspaper I saw in Rolf's house. Directly across the square from the ice cream shop, the library's stone pillars and carved wooden doors make it the grandest building in town. The sign out front explains that they're not open in the evenings, Saturday afternoons, or Sundays from June through August. *I guess only the unemployed can check books out in the summer,* I think to myself.

I pull open the door. It takes a moment for my eyes to adjust. I spot the librarian, scanning in returns behind the desk. She wears a turtleneck and a sweatshirt decorated with embroidered autumn leaves, despite the warm weather. "And how can I help you today?" she asks. She slips her glasses off and I worry she's dropped them, but they halt at the end of a string of beads around her neck. From a distance, I'd assumed her to be older. With the glasses off, I see she's probably about my age.

"Do you know how I might go about searching old issues of the local newspaper?"

She tilts her head. "I'm afraid we haven't digitized any of that." She picks up the next book from the stack of returns as if our business were through.

"That's fine. Microfiche or microfilm—do you have it in one of those formats?"

"Yes, but I'd need to find someone who knows how to use the machine." She doesn't move.

"Great. Could you please do that?"

Her smile widens, a practiced way of scowling with no evidence. She disappears into the office behind the reference desk and procures an older, mustachioed gentleman. He eyes me up and down, and I remember we're in a small town and remind myself to be surprised this doesn't happen more often.

"I hear you want to look at old newspapers. Why's that?"

I explain we've just moved here and I'm interested in researching some history in the town. He points to a thin volume with a poorly designed cover on the "Local Interest" display nearby. "That'll tell you everything you need to know."

I thank him and say I'll check it out. "My interests are a bit more specific, though." I smile more than I normally do to try to put him at ease. I wonder if all the teeth make me look like a maniac, the way Julie grinned at the high school student working at the hardware store.

He leads me down to the basement, to a dim corner of plastic machines yellowed with age. "I keep pushing to have these files updated and backed up. If there were a fire, we'd lose all of these records. Not to mention, you're the first one in ages who's been willing to learn how to use this equipment. Usually people say, 'Forget it!' But the machines are actually quite easy to use. Now, what year did you want to look at?"

I realize now that I don't know. "The forties?"

The librarian chuckles and pats me on the back. "You'll need to narrow it down a bit, son. Where would you like to start?"

I tell him I'll start with 1940, and he goes to retrieve the reels. I find I can scan rather quickly with only fifty-two head-lines per year. I browse 1941 and 1942 with no luck, but 1943 turns up what I'm looking for.

KINSLER FAMILY TRAGEDY

CASEVILLE, Wis.—An eight-year-old boy from Caseville died Tuesday after falling 50 feet from a tree. Kent County deputies said Alban Kinsler was playing with his six-year-old brother, Rolf, in the Harper Woods behind their home at 891 Stillwater Lane, 3:15 p.m., Tuesday. The brothers climbed a tree and Alban fell to the dirt ground below when a branch weakened by white rot gave way. Rolf was unharmed. The boys' mother, Bette, happened to be watch-ing from their kitchen window when it happened. Alban Kinsler was taken to Caseville County Hospital, where doc-tors were unable to revive the boy. He was pronounced dead at 4:10 p.m.

A wake was held at Christ Lutheran Church, where mourners stretched around the block, waiting to pay their respects to Mr. and Mrs. Kinsler and the little boy's brother. The family has requested privacy.

I note the address as Rolf's house, not our own, as I worried it might be. I think of the portrait above the mantel of his house that showed a son and a daughter and wonder if I'd misread the picture. Maybe it was two sons, and the baby was wearing a baptismal gown. I remember old photos of little boys with long hair and frocklike garments.

I ask the librarian if I can print the article, and he shows me how. When he sees the page I'm interested in copying, he asks what I'm researching.

"The house next door to ours."

"I see. You're in the house almost identical to the Kinsler house, then? Eight ninety-five? I didn't realize anyone had moved in there." He opens his mouth to continue. I see the words reroute themselves. "Welcome to town." He leaves it at that.

He starts to unload the cartridge from the machine. I stop him. "I'd like to continue poking around a bit if it's not too much trouble."

"None at all. I'll leave you to it."

I scan through more slowly now, reading the headlines on the inner pages. I want to see if I can find anything more. No stories provide an update on the family in 1943. I ask the librarian if I can see the following year's reel. He tells me I'll have to come back another day. He's heading out. No one else knows how to operate the machine. I'm irked that he won't load one more file for me before he goes. I tell him I understand, though. I thank him for his help.

I take my leave of the library and drive away. When I see the pull-off into the woods north of our home, I make a split-second decision and veer in. Three other cars are parked in the small lot. I notice a man sits at the steering wheel in each one. I wonder what they're waiting for. I walk east to the shore and then south, hoping to find a path that will loop back west so I can explore more rather than retracing my steps. As the daylight fades, I'm about to resign myself to turning around when I realize I'm higher above the water than I think. I reorient myself. I figure out I'm above the cave we've noticed north of our beach. I step-slide my way down to the entrance. I don't think about how I'll get back up. I duck into the grotto. I hear the dripping around me and look back out, unsure I should go farther inside. A sheer drop leads to the surf below. The light travels only as far as the shallow parts of the cave. In the dark, I can see writing and drawings on the wall. The layers of scribbling grow denser as I venture farther back. I cannot make any of it out. My eyes exhaust themselves. I hunt my pockets for my phone, but can't find it. I wish I had my camera.

I look around the mouth of the cave to assess how I'll get off the cliff. The trees above are spindly, held down by weak, rocky soil. I have nothing with which to lasso them. It starts to drizzle. I argue with myself if it would be better to make a go of the climb now, just as the rocks are getting slippery, or if I should wait to see if the rain clouds pass before the sun sets. I take a seat inside the lip of the cave. I lean against the rock. I close my eyes. I wait for an idea. When I open my eyes again, I am dozing in my rocking chair on the front of our wraparound porch. I ask Julie where I've been. She laughs. She tells me I haven't moved from that chair since I got home from the library, even when she asked me if I wanted to go for a walk on the beach with her. I start to explain what I found out about the Kinslers.

She stops me. "You told me all of this when you got home."

I am afraid to admit I don't remember. Like a blacked-out drunk trying to cover for himself, I say, "Of course I did. I know."

23

WHEN ANOTHER BRUISE appears down the length of my shin, I go to the doctor and he tells me I'm dangerously low on an array of vitamins. He writes down, "Iron, B, D, and E in concentrated doses," and hands me the slip of paper.

I buy the vitamins and swallow them down each day, but the bruises still come. My inner thighs look as if they've been pummeled so I stop going to the beach to walk or swim and start wearing sweatpants to work because everything hurts. I stop James on his way to the living room and lift up my shirt to show him the bruise leaking down my chest, bleeding from my sternum to my belly button, and James says, "When did that one show up?"

"Today."

He reaches out toward the bruise, placing his palm flat against me, gently, the bronze of his hand contrasting with my pale stomach, and the spot gets warm, as if his hand were a heating pad, and he pushes against my ribs a little harder, and the hum in the air swells louder, and it looks as if the bones were folding in, as if they'd turned to clay, but they don't feel that way. It feels as if I'm getting better, stronger.

When he pulls his hand away, the ribs slowly rise again, like memory foam, and I tell myself the answer is breath.

24

"THEY SHOULD BE able to diagnose this, right? Bruises seem like a pretty straightforward symptom," I say.

Julie leans down to turn another shovelful of dirt. "But I wonder how many times a physician is certain of his diagnosis and it's actually wrong. I'd prefer no diagnosis to a wrong one." She tugs with all her might at a plant whose leaves look like the blade of a saw. "This is a weed, right?" She answers her own question and pulls.

I glance around the yard. "Anything I can do?"

"Out here? Not yet. You can mow the lawn later. For now, you can start painting or you can replace the hardware on the sinks."

"I can paint, but I think we need to call a plumber to do the other stuff."

"Fine. Remember to tape all along the ceiling and baseboards . . . doors . . . windows."

With one last tug, the roots of the plant show themselves. The fist of white tentacles is covered in dirt. It's bigger, more bulbous, than I expected.

I try to remember what paint color goes where. The cans and supplies have been piled in the entryway since we returned from the hardware store. "Maybe we could paint together, though? I worry I'll do the tape wrong."

Julie stops for a moment, frustrated that I can't take care of this on my own. She knows I'm right, though. "How about you finish pulling weeds, and I'll get started taping?"

She is missing the point. I want us to be together, but I accept her offer. Flora is something I do know. Julie hands me her gloves. She turns to head inside.

"Wait." I grab her around the waist. I kiss her. She kisses me back. When we pull away, her face shines ruddy with exertion.

"Thank you." The smile fades fast as she focuses behind me. "Again!"

I follow her eyes to Rolf at his window, holding a mug. He looks as though he's stopping on his way somewhere else. I wave. He doesn't respond.

"I wonder how long he's been watching," Julie says, staring back.

"It doesn't matter," I say. "He doesn't matter."

25

I TAKE AN afternoon off. I tell Sam and Kim I have a doctor's appointment back in the city. I complain about not having found someone local yet. Really, though, I head for the art museum to see a photography exhibit I missed before we moved. I don't tell Julie. She'd be angry I'm using a vacation day. She'd try to tell me that I shouldn't take a day off so soon after starting this new job. She'd want to come along. But I need an afternoon alone. I plan to get there and back in the span of the workday. That leaves me about two hours of museum time.

I spend the drive there clearing my head. I watch the rural farms turn to suburbs and then city gridlock.

In the modern wing, I stand before a black-and-white photo of a gentleman wrapped in thick foam. The material is what you'd use as a mattress if you didn't have the time to save for springs and feathers. His head cranes back as if he's bothered by something. He smokes. A long clothbound electrical cord winds through his arms, draped on the foam. Concrete walls him in.

I think about how smoking is a way of trying to satisfy each moment. It disregards the future. How many cigarettes must this man have already smoked? How many more will he smoke in his lifetime? Is there a way all the filters could connect end to end to bridge the gap between this man and me? This man— who I've assumed lives across the ocean because of the information on the placard—and I could be united by some superglue that would bind his cigarette filters together. They'd stretch up and over the ocean. Some magical force would suspend them. I know, though, that the shape of the earth would refuse this happening. I will never find this man. I will never ask him what was bothering him. My breath rushes in and out. Did this man make it through whatever issue caused his mouth to jack into such a sprawling smile? Neck strung tight. I want to tell that man that the smoke will never fill him up. Nothing will. The yellowing it leaves behind will get closer and darker. The thing he's trying to expand will shrink into nothing. What he's found is a way to close in on himself. I stand in front of that print. Sweat prickles my skin. A photo is reflections of light. Everything invisible comes together to show you something. My throat constricts. I start to laugh. My chest feels snug. A security guard comes closer. I lose my balance and vision and sound.

I wake up on a gurney, but refuse to go to the hospital. An EMT says into my cell phone, "Okay, he's coming to, I'm going to put him on."

It's Julie. She wants to know if I'm okay. "What happened? Why are you all the way in the city?"

It takes a little while for me to even think of what the truth is, let alone a lie that would make everything seem normal.

I wait in the lobby for her to make it to me. She and Connie pull up. Connie will drive Julie's car home so Julie can drive mine. As Julie climbs the big flight of stairs out front, I see her wave Connie off. Already Julie's eyes search through the glass doors for me. She tugs them open and struts toward me. She pulls me up to standing. She hugs me. I hug her back. I can feel everyone watching: the guards and every set of eyes in every painting. I want to tell her, *I'm fine.* And *It was nothing.* And *I should have eaten something more.* I can't lie. I say, "Let's go."

On the way home, Julie talks nonstop. I try to listen. I still feel a bit woozy. My head aches.

"Why would you do that?"

In the question, I hear what she's not asking: *Did you actually go up to the city to gamble, to join the old crew at the bar, to lay what little money you've earned in the last month down?* I feel the anger growing in me that her concern for my well-being is being overridden by her suspicion.

"It was a bad idea. Okay? I don't feel well right now. Can you save the lecture?"

Julie keeps quiet then. She doesn't apologize. She allows me to drift off.

26

AFTER WE RETURN from the museum, James sleeps for twenty-four hours until he wakes, distant and paranoid. He says he wants to change things, wants to get to the root of whatever it is that's filling the spaces of this house. I think he means this abstractly, but then he begins unscrewing switch plates, he pulls out the stove, runs his hand under the cabinets, climbs onto a stepladder to remove the ceiling vents. Beneath the surface of it all, we discover more ligament than we imagined, but the rudiments of the house aren't what James is looking for. It's something else that I can't figure out. "James, what is it you think you'll find?"

"If I knew, I wouldn't be looking."

James makes a precise cut along the edge of the box spring and inspects each coil. He removes the stuffing from the sofa cushions and rips open the seams on the pillows. He tries to settle the feathers in a neat pile, but they take flight in a panic when I enter the room. "I'll put them back," he says.

James pulls up the edge of the carpet to show me the grime hiding between it and the floorboards, and I force the corner back down. I can't let myself think about the dirt hiding where we can't get to it. I heave at the thought of the filth caked into this old house. "You can't make a shell of our home, James." I try to trace this destruction to the way he picked horses and hoped they'd win. I tell myself people can have two problems with no common cause. He drills a hole in the wall between the two bedrooms, trying to get to that oddly shaped void we'd originally thought was a closet.

When an opening big enough for a flashlight is formed, he shines the light in and tells me, "It's just an empty column of space. It goes pretty far up and down."

I peek in. "Maybe it was a laundry chute or a dumbwaiter? Maybe they sealed it off when they stopped using it."

James says, "I don't know where else to look. Where is the sound coming from? The moisture? Your bruises? I can't find it."

I try to stay calm and stroke his back and tell him maybe there's nothing to be found.

That night, we lie on our mattress, tufts of stuffing pulled out and resting beside us on the ground, exhausted and uncomfortable, but unwilling to do the work of filling it back up, the springs digging into our backs more accurate, more true.

27

I WAKE UP early and feel nothing. I go back to sleep. I wake up again. I feel the pressure. Remorse stings through me, like a hangover without having had a drink. I remember slowly. I look at the seams sliced into all of our belongings. Screws balance on every surface. I see an exaggeration of some impulse that is familiar to me. I see what I've done with surprise, but unearth no doubt.

I emptied everything I could find in the house. I worry Julie will identify this as a ripple of what I did with my bank account. I gambled enough away that the money still remaining only reminded me of what I'd lost and so I gambled that away, too.

Now it is my job to refill what I've emptied. I sew it all shut. I drill every screw back into place. I make dinner: grilled fillets and asparagus, my only culinary talent.

Julie returns home relieved to see order restored. We sit down at the table. Julie eats without a word. She doesn't look at me until her plate is clean. "Well, that was a real fast one-two punch. First the museum and then cutting everything apart, but that's it, right? We're not headed down some irreversible path? Can I help? Do you want to talk to someone?"

"I don't know what came over me," I say. "The incident at the museum unmoored me, but I feel better today."

Julie's eyes are filling up. She shuts them lightly. She tries not to let the tears spill. "James, if it happens again, I need to tell someone. I need to get us help."

I feel incapable of facing the worry I've caused her. My mind insists that her recent transgressions have been more severe than my own. "We need to watch out for each other is all. I'll do the dishes. You go relax." I stand to gather our plates. Julie wanders to the couch. She stares at the television as if she can see something in its blank screen. I finish the dishes and hear the stairs creak.

I try to make it up to her. I wipe down the counter. I take the trash out. The moon is low. I have to search for it. The woods seem closer than they had earlier that day. I count my paces to their edge. Fifty in all, though I swear it used to be a hundred.

Back in the house, I shake my shoes off inside the door. I head upstairs. When I pass the guest room, I see Julie sitting in the dark wearing an old Mardi Gras mask we'd brought home from vacation once upon a time. "What are you doing in there?"

She whispers, "Nothing." I barely hear it. I exhale a short laugh. I keep moving to our bedroom.

"What am I doing in where?" Julie says from our bed. She is tucked in tight, book in hand. I startle when I see her. I return to the guest room. The mask is back on the wall.

I check the closet. I find it empty. I insist on maintaining Julie's confidence and so I return to our bedroom and say, "Oh, I'm tired. Just being silly." I shut the bedroom door. Julie raises her eyebrows at the click of the lock. I pull on my pajamas. My skin feels warm and tight, as if it's been burned. I know that isn't something the moon can do.

28

AT WORK, I take Connie to lunch and we sit at a table on the sidewalk in front of the restaurant near the train station. We split a bottle of white and order the daily catch.

"It's like an exclusionary diagnosis," I tell her. "It's maddening. How can I accept that the solution is just all the things it's not? That means there's no answer."

Connie squints. "What are we talking about? The bruises? Or James? The house?"

"All of the above? The symptoms keep adding up. I wonder about selling the house and going back to the city, but what if that's not the answer and then we've gone to all that trouble? I'm not willing to give up on this place yet."

"I hear you, hon, but we've got to improve this situation for you. Leave the house or get James in to see a counselor or both."

"Yeah," I say, "but I'm at fault, too. I've got the bruises and sometimes I feel so out of it, like I'm miles away. There are times I completely understand how he's thinking about things, you know? I get it."

"Right, but empathy can only take you so far. You've got to have a little objective distance, too, so you can see what needs to change."

The food arrives and we dig into our fish platters, dip broccoli in tartar sauce, stay quiet for a few minutes. "I understand what you're saying. I want to think through everything really carefully."

"Have you mentioned any of it to your parents? Or to his?"

"No! I mean, my stepmother thinks the house needs to be exorcised, but it's hard to take her opinion seriously." I don't want to tell Connie about the sounds we heard when my parents visited. I wipe my hands in my napkin. "James's parents would whisk him home if they knew how he'd been behaving. My dad and stepmother would be out here in a minute filing lawsuits and having James committed and admitting me to Mayo. Maybe they'd all be in the right, but I don't think we're quite at that point."

The train goes by and I take the opportunity to chew and evaluate Connie's reaction. I can feel her forming an allegiance, convinced this is James's fault. It feels more like something in the space between James and me, though, like an electricity that's been turned on since we've taken up this new life, something that buzzes at its highest frequency when we're both home, together. I go along with the idea that James might be the biggest part of the problem so that I don't scare Connie off. I need her right now.

When the quiet is restored, Connie says, "You know the situation better than me, so I won't pretend I can give you advice. Say the word if you need help, though."

"This is all the help I need." I drain my wine and Connie refills my glass.

29

WHEN WE LOOK for the house on a map, we see only a black square.

When we seek out the woods: cross-hatching.

When we hunt for the lake, we find a watermark.

Every map.

At work, Sam asks me what's wrong.

"Julie's mad at me. I fucked up. I don't know what to do other than apologize." I pull out my chair.

"You cheat on her?" he asks, spinning around. His chair squeaks so loudly I wince.

"No, nothing like that."

Sam shrugs. "What's she doing?"

I wonder what it is that allows me to keep placing a frame around the parts I want to hide. "She's not doing anything really. It's not the silent treatment because she's talking to me, but it feels like that."

"Well, here's a thought: Why don't you ask her what's up?" he says.

"I think she'll ignore me. She'll pretend like nothing's wrong."

"I'm no Dr. Phil, James, but I'm pretty sure you should give her the benefit of the doubt and wait for her behavior to improve. Am I right? Chances are she'll get tired of being angry. But maybe she can tell you what she's still holding on to. Talk to her." Sam raises his eyebrows.

"So logical. Out of nowhere, you're logical." I turn back to my screen.

"I do what I can," he says.

In the last hour of the day, I start getting texts every few minutes from Julie:

"James."

"James."

"James."

"James."

"James."

"James."

I don't respond. I think it's a duplicate, some cellular glitch. Maybe she's being antsy. I don't want to get into a texting war. I want a chance to talk to her in person before anything else goes off.

At 4:59, the message changes: "For real. I need help."

I call her. "What's wrong, Julie?"

She is silent for a long time. "I'm stuck in some room of the house. I don't know how to get out."

"I'll be right home," I say.

I gather my coat. Sam asks if I finished up the project I'd been working on. I tell him, "Cover for me."

30

I HEAR THE door slam, feel the reverberations. When I dial James's phone, the call goes straight to voice mail. I crouch down to see if there's a lip between the floor and the wall to grab and shove out, but instead I find a book, leatherbound and wedged thick with loose pages. The room seems to pull in closer, and I panic, wondering if I'll be crushed, then suddenly the wall behind me slides to one side on its own, and light floods in and I am in our bedroom, and I push through the crack quickly, and I look at where I've been and it's just another space we don't know, a narrow closet, and I examine how the wall works and slide it back, trying not to close it completely, but it clicks into place and then I can't seem to budge it open again. I try to crank the wall sconce and step gingerly in different areas of the floor to see if I can trigger the opening again, but to no effect. In the light of the room, the book in my hand seems to be a journal and my instinct is to keep it for myself and

I wonder why I am turning it into another secret even as I stuff it into the drawer of the nightstand and collapse onto the bed.

James comes into the room, screaming for me, then quieting down when he sees I am right here. "Where were you? What happened?"

I smile because I always smile when I shouldn't, a nervous tic. I point to the wall that has resealed itself and then open my hand up and raise my eyebrows.

"What do you mean?"

"There's a room behind that wall, but it's gone now."

He looks at me strangely. "There can't be. It's the guest room on the other side. There's not enough space."

I'm too tired to convince him. "Well, I didn't make it up."

I can tell he wonders if this is all a bid for attention, if I was ever even trapped. "Talk to me, Julie. What's going on? Are you mad at me? Are you trying to get back at me?"

I don't know.

31

WE GO ABOUT our evening, making dinner and rummaging about the house. I try to keep up a regular conversation, but James clips his responses. He takes a call from his parents. "I know you want to visit, but now isn't a good time. Julie's under the weather. We'll let you know as soon as we get settled . . . Just a cold, I think . . . I will . . . Love you, too. Bye." I snuggle into him while he watches the news, tuck into his armpit, and wrap an arm around the pudge of his belly, and he allows it, but after about ten minutes he tells me he's wiped and heads upstairs to bed.

I cry on the couch, feeling the gap that's formed between us widening when we'd hoped this move would close it. I cycle three times through all the channels before I give up.

The lights in the bedroom are off. In the soft shine of the moon through the window, I startle at what looks like a person opposite me, only to realize it's a figure drawn on the wall. I flip my bedside light on, not sure if I hope to wake James or not. The outline droops with liquid, watery and pink, and I wonder, *Paint? Blood?* Those are all of the answers I can think of.

I remember the drawings on the wall the lady at the grocery store told me about. I shiver at this form, crude—like a child's sketch: a rough, wide oval for its head; limbs that stretch too long; features simple and too small for the face.

James and I are living in a Latin mass, memorizing ritual, reciting mysteries we've given up on deciphering, foreign syllables unrolling in order.

I want to flip the light on and scream. I want to rock James awake and say, *James, you said this was over* and also *I feel like something's gone wrong in me,* but instead I crawl under the blanket with him and place a hand on his smooth back and rest my lips on his shoulder and I pray.

32

"I GOT A talking-to from Kim," I tell Sam. He's eating a left-over pulled-pork sandwich at 9:05 a.m. I can see he's already kicked his shoes off under his desk.

"Ah, I'm sorry, man. I couldn't stay late last night. It would have taken me all night to get caught up with where you were in the project, and I had dinner plans." He holds up the sandwich as if it's evidence.

"It's cool. I should have come back after I ran home."

"Everything okay with Julie?" A piece of pork falls into his lap. He picks it up and delivers it into his mouth. The grease stain it leaves behind on his pants goes untended.

"I don't know." I edit my reply carefully. "She, uh, got stuck in a closet yesterday. How does that happen? And then I found this weird drawing on the wall of our bedroom."

"Some crafty shit? Leaves and birds? My mom did that once and my dad painted over it because it was so bad. She was *pissed*."

"No. I'm not sure what she was after with this. It's like a cartoon person."

"That'd be cool. Like Wolverine busting through the wall?"

I don't correct him. I turn my computer on and take a sip of coffee.

Sam shifts. "Boss lady was mad, though, huh?"

"I shouldn't ask for special treatment. They don't even know me yet. I get it. It felt like an emergency. How do you explain that your wife somehow got lost in your own house? I know that sounds crazy."

I've already spent Sam's attention, though. He chuckles a little too late. I can tell he's been absorbed into his computer screen.

33

I BEAT JAMES home from work, and instead of starting dinner as I normally would, I put on sneakers and walk across the yard. I listen for the children or for the birds, but I'm unspecific about my listening, and I can't tell which it is I hear far out in the distance.

The day is clear and so the water reflects blue when I emerge on the beach. I feel hunger thrum within me and regret not cooking right away, and so I turn around. I retract back home, on automatic, my attention focused only on the ground in front of me. I emerge on the other side of the woods and cross through the grass and pull open the back door and find myself not in our home, but in Rolf's kitchen. The door slams behind me, and I freeze, shocked, uncertain how I could be where I am, asking myself if this is the first time this has happened or the second. I force myself to move forward into his living room and pause to look at the portrait above the fireplace and search the young boy's face for a resemblance to Rolf and find that familiar underbite, jutting out farther even than his wide, broken-looking nose. On the couch, I see a sweater that looks like one of my own. A reflex makes my hand grab it and hold it up and the label is the same brand as mine, a size large, but the knit has a stiff spot, like a liquid has dried near the collar. Cat hair snarls on the side that was facing out. When I hold the cardigan to my face, the smell of ammonia repels me. I vise the sweater between two fingers and tear the front door open, unconcerned about Rolf's hearing the noise. I beat a shortcut through the fountain grass lining his front walk and yank open our own door and deposit the sweater in the laundry room before I run up the stairs to our bedroom, collapse facedown on the bed, deafen my exasperation in a pillow, and come up for air, certain the scent of that sweater is still straying nearby. Did Rolf steal my cardigan? Why? Had I been in his house before? Had I left it there? For a moment, I let myself consider what it must be like for an old man to hear his own front door slam and not know who or what has caused it. What role were we playing? The ghosts or the haunted?

When I look up, the figure drawn on the bedroom wall seems bigger than the night before, but I don't yield to the confusion this time. I trace its edges with permanent marker to track growth, trying to define my own standard of safety.

I pull the journal I'd found in the wall out of the bedside table. I flick through, and illegible writing fills the pages—tiny, layered, crisscrossed—each piece of paper a woven tapestry. The penmanship forms itself like a rolling wave, never peaking or breaking. Stuffed into the beginning, some loose pages appear more precise but uncertain, like the handwriting of a child.

Mother avoids me now that Alban is gone. The shades stay drawn and I'm to be quiet. The people at church pity us. We hear them whispering. *It's unfortunate. I can't imagine. Where was she at the time? I would have been there.*

Father tells Mother they'll have another child when the time is right. Mother wants another child *now*. Every night she cries.

At dinner now, we don't speak. I stare straight ahead. Tonight, Mother broke the silence with Alban's name. Mother struck herself. She slammed her head onto the table, punched her belly, bit her lip, squeezed the flesh of her legs so hard beneath her fingers that bruises formed. Father clutched her. I sit outside the closed loop of them. I am not enough.

Father disappears for days at a time. Mother's sloppy grief has turned tough. He runs away. Mother is furious. Everything is worse.

At suppertime, I shave valerian root into the pots on the stove, trying to put all of us to sleep. I hide from her nightmares, stuff a blanket under the door, hum, make all the noise I can to block out the sounds. I can see her bad moods coming and swerve to avoid them.

I hear James arrive home. I force the book back into the drawer and lie down. He enters the room and rifles through the dresser for sweatpants. "Just taking a rest before dinner," I say, as if he's asked for an answer. He looks at the drawing, then at me. He gets out his camera and snaps several exposures.

"Not a bad idea," I say, "to start documenting your work."

He looks at me with a smirk I don't recognize. I expect James to apologize or explain, but nothing of that sort emerges.

The nights like this start to line up like matchsticks, close together, hard to count.

34

I USUALLY LOVE the dark, but on this night, it is not my friend and it feels like a punishment to be forced to sit in the pitch and stare. The pages inserted into the journal talk about the death of a brother. I think of what James told me about Rolf's family losing a son and decide I need to tell him what I've found. Why is the book in our house, though? James said they weren't living in this house when Alban died, but had they lived here at some other point? These preoccupations twist themselves out of the darkness. I watch them tick by like seconds on a clock. I tell myself that all this night is, is a bunch of instants, and even when you add them up, it's not that much, and finally I fall half-asleep, but James and I startle awake at the same moment, both listening for that growl we'd heard, but it's not a sound. Something else has fussed us. James tells me he had a dream that a girl wouldn't stop climbing on top of him, shouting in his face. I tell him that an identical dream woke me.

I huddle into James, still comforted by the way I can tuck perfectly into his big frame, and I breathe in the scent of his sleep-soaked neck and smell love and grief, like chicory.

James pounds his fist into the mattress and pulls away and shouts, "What the hell? It's too much." I feel comforted that at least he believes me, that he doesn't think I've made up my duplicate version of his dream. I think about telling him about the book, too, but I don't want to turn the light on. I don't want to lose hours of sleep to paging through the journal together now; I want him to know what I know as soon as I know it. This dream is already too much and impatience sparks within me like a menace, threatening to catch. I tell myself, *Tomorrow.*

I can't stop the tears that dash down my face quietly. I keep them secret until James kisses my cheek and tastes the briny gloss and squeezes tighter so that eventually I calm down, but I don't hear our breaths fall into the pattern of sleep.

In the morning the birches all hunch at the edge of the yard, groggy, as if they, too, were up all night, and we are on the other side of half-awake, James looking dried out, a salted version of himself.

Every time a door in the house creaks, it says something a little different, and like those picture puzzles where you have to find the errors, we can't pinpoint it, but we hear the something that is off.

In the cupboard, all the jars of pickled and jellied things are empty, but unclean, as though someone has been eating them and then shoving the hollowed vessels to the back, until the empties have nothing to hide behind. The clock on the wall of the kitchen stopped days ago, and I can't reach it, but I wouldn't know where to move the hands anyway.

Every time I look at the neighbor's house, he's staring back: Who's checking up on whom?

35

IN THE MORNING, a fresh drawing of peacocks on the wall next to the last one. A new figure. "What is this?" I ask. Julie looks away. "Does it mean anything?" I can sense her nerves. I take more photos.

"Look at this." Julie's hand is stretched around a leather-bound book stuffed with paper. "I found it in the wall when I was stuck. It's a journal, but look at the writing: it's those layers people have been mentioning, that that girl wrote in. But then, back here, the handwriting's different."

She hands me the book and I flip through. The pages of plaited script aren't readable, but the short excerpts written in a messier, more childlike hand are.

Mother is still beautiful, but her heart thumps, wet and heavy. I hear it in my ears. When I see her, my fingertips tingle. Last night, I watched her turn the lamps off, and her skin gripped some of that light, even in the dark.

At breakfast today, I watched Mother disappear. The sunlight shined around her and half of her face faded out. She stares at me. She thinks I pushed Alban from the tree.

Tonight, by the fire, mother could not keep herself awake. Her eyes look snuffed out. I tried to tell her about my time in the woods, but she responded only with taut nodding, drowsy. She asked the same question over and over, "How did you spend your day?" like I hadn't already answered.

Mother may be an impostor. Perhaps she's been replaced.

I read in my detectives' book that no two ears shape themselves the same way, like fingerprints. I examined earlier photographs of my mother. I searched for one that showed the outline of her ear and memorized the curls. Sitting beside her, though, I'm disappointed to see her ears remain the same.

Mother keeps a copy of Alban's birth certificate by her rocking chair in the front window and stares at it. The blue of her eyes seems clearer now, as if too much light has gotten in. I would like to tear that piece of paper apart.

Father has been gone for days. A week? The longest yet. Would it be better if I ran away, too?

"Is this Rolf, do you think? How did it get into our house?" Julie looks as if she's not yet woken up. Her eye makeup is smudged, her skin is slick with the oiled swell of morning. "I don't know. Maybe they lived in this house first? Then moved next door? Or maybe they lived there and then moved here and Rolf moved back?"

"And the other writing? Have you been able to decipher any of it?"

"I haven't tried." Julie hoists herself up and exits the room. "I have to get to work."

I follow her. She doesn't stop in the kitchen. She opens the front door to let herself out. "Julie, are you going to shower? Change your clothes?"

She looks up at me, one hand on the knob. "I know what I look like," she says, as if her appearance were an unchangeable fact. In that moment, I trust her expertise. She closes the door.

I make myself coffee. I tell myself that if I stick around here, I can hunt this book for answers. That's more important than work. I pause and say, "This should be a big deal. Maybe reconsider." Not calling in is grounds for immediate termination, but I take the chance.

I return upstairs.

Last night, I found Mother's teeth in a dish on the bathroom sink. I went to their bedroom to ask about them, and their door was open. I heard only breath, like pistons firing. I saw the back of Father's head. "Mother?" I said, and her head fell to the side to look at me, but what I saw can't be true: she had no face. I recall the outline of her jaw and her mussed hair, but no features. When she said my name, I didn't see her lips move. I ran back to the bathroom and cried. I wanted to dash her wretched teeth to the ground. This morning Mother scolded me for having gotten out of bed in the night.

The paper changed from a creamy stationery to a flimsier onionskin.

Eleanor Marie born at 9:45 a.m. Tuesday. She is too small and wiggly for me to hold her. Her eyes dart around like a lizard's. If I give her my finger, she holds on tightly. Even when she sleeps, she jolts. Mother wonders when she will calm down.

Eleanor makes all sorts of noises. I think I can understand her, but Mother says that's impossible.

Mother compares Eleanor to Alban constantly, talking about when Alban was a newborn. I watch the way Father stares at Mother feeding Eleanor. He has not been leaving as often, thank goodness. When I am alone with Eleanor, I tell her I will always look after her and give her guidance. This is the role of a big brother.

And then the neatly written entries end. I scan through the pages of layered text, but time has lightened and smeared the graphite so that it looks less like letters and more like a pattern, unreadable. I blur my eyes, looking for a hidden message. I remember from my childhood the shape of a dolphin forming from a stereogram. No such resolution is revealed, though. I put the book onto Julie's bedside table. I head down to the basement to develop some photos. I try to see what it is I've been looking at.

36

"WHAT'S WRONG with you?" Connie says. "Why do you look like that?"

I touch my hair delicately. "Like what?" I can feel the tangles beneath my palm.

She lowers her voice. "Your hair is all mashed onto one side of your head, and—I'm sorry—I'm only telling you because I'd expect you to do the same for me, but you smell awful. Like urine, maybe?"

I sniff at my arms and ask myself, *How long does it take to become immune to a smell, to trouble?*

"Julie, we're supposed to meet with the investors this afternoon. Did you forget?"

"No," I say. "Why?"

"Tim, Julie and I are taking a personal hour, okay? We'll be back soon." Our colleague raises his eyebrows and Connie rolls her eyes and takes me by the arm. "Let's get you cleaned up," she whispers in my ear, and I don't resist.

She unlocks the car doors and says, "Wait." She pulls an old camping blanket from the trunk and places it on the passenger seat before she'll let me sit. "Okay. Go ahead . . . You in? Watch your elbow." She shuts the door.

On the way to the house, Connie asks me all sorts of questions that don't seem to matter, and then we pull up and I follow Connie to the porch. "Okay, open her up," she says.

I stare at her.

"Where's your purse?" she asks.

I shake my head.

37

"COME IN!" I shout from the darkroom. They don't hear me.

I wash the fixer off the photo I've been developing. I hang it to dry. I worry about being found out. Julie will be furious I'm not at my office. She won't accuse me of anything before she checks the bank accounts. If I say I feel sick, it wouldn't be untrue. I consider staying in the basement. Maybe they're just stopping home to pick something up. Maybe they're grabbing an early lunch. I hear two sets of feet climb the stairs to the second floor. I lose track of their voices beneath the hum of the house.

I lean in to look at the picture I've just clipped to the line. The tree trunks cluster in a row like tick marks on a timeline. I look in the branches for anything. I try to remember what I was trying to record when I'd snapped the photo. I think about how to help her. Julie, the dedicated perfectionist, was known for following through. But now, all of her patterns have splayed into chaos. The balance of our collective reliability has been thrown off. If she's not in charge, no one is.

I crawl out of the basement. Worry at how long I'd need to hide down there powers my movement. I reach the top of the second-floor stairs, undetected. I pause outside the door. I lean against the wall. I am afraid I've waited too long now to let them know I'm here.

Connie says, "This place is a mess. I'm sorry, but it is." Julie doesn't argue. She says nothing. I consider breaking in, but Connie goes on. "Schmutz pact, but it reeks in here. Do you remember what a schmutz pact is? Like if you have a little dirt on your face, as a true friend, I will tell you so you can take care of it, rather than letting you walk around like that." She coughs. "Don't look at me with those big eyes. Fix this place. I'm a friend, and I'm giving it to you straight. Figure out where that smell is coming from. Let's get you into the bathtub."

I pivot my body into the doorway. "Hey—"

Connie screams. She bumps into the dresser behind her. She grabs at her spine where it caught the corner. "James! Jesus Christ! Have you been here the whole time? Holy fuck." She leans on the dresser. She looks at Julie. Julie hasn't said a thing. She hasn't even looked at me. Connie notices this. She examines my face. She waits for an explanation. She waits for one of us to own up to something.

"I'm sorry, I was down in the darkroom. Why are you home? Is everything okay?"

Connie's breath is still working itself out. I watch her nostrils expand and contract. I can see her collarbone flare into view. "That explains why the door was unlocked. We need to clean Julie up. Wouldn't you agree?"

I nod tentatively, unsure if this will elicit a reaction from Julie.

"Why are *you* home?" Connie asks me.

I panic and lie, "Oh, to let in an electrician." I wait for a moment that I can walk away to make a call, to make the story true.

"Oh, yeah? Julie, did you know an electrician was coming today?" Julie remains still. Connie glares at me, as if Julie's behavior were my fault.

The two of them disappear behind the door. I wish I'd told Connie I could take care of Julie myself. It feels too late. It feels like help we need.

38

CONNIE RUNS THE bath and undresses me and I don't wonder why James isn't the one doing this and I let Connie see the bruises newly formed near my ankles and along my armpit. "Let's be real here," she whispers, as she holds my arm and I lower into the warm water. "Is he hurting you?"

"No."

"Then what is it?"

I think of James's overdrawn account, of the slow suspicion that grew when I saw the ATM withdrawals from our joint checking, small sums—twenty or forty dollars—amounts that he would normally have taken out of his private funds, until he couldn't. Of how I ignored it for a while until the frequency increased and I asked if he'd gotten his ATM cards confused and how James had broken down and told me what had happened, of how he had started visiting the OTB on his lunch hour, laying down cash on races, forming what felt like friendships with the other guys urging their workday along with a shot of adrenaline at noon, ordering hot wings and beer as an alibi. I think of the cave James is convinced he visited, of all he's dismantled, and I remember that I have no answer for where the bruises come from or for where I disappeared to when the house swallowed me up, and we have no explanation for the noises— the intonation or the deep breathing in the night or the voices looting our dreams—and no reasons for the drawings or the children in the woods, things we see together, even if we're apart. My instinct is to pin the trouble on James, but I ask myself if it might be easier to believe it's neither of us, so that we might trust each other and try to solve this mystery together.

Connie sits on the toilet, and I think about whether she noticed how much the bathwater rose when I sat down in it. It's something I'd worried about since I was a teenager, the serenity of a bath marred by my anxiety about my own volume. She is so thin, so elegantly formed. I feel certain she knows the water she'd displace wouldn't be more than an inch or two.

"You don't have to talk to me. I know we might not be as close as I feel like we are. We haven't kept in touch. We've only just reconnected. But I hope you're talking to *someone*." Connie stares straight ahead, trying not to look at my body.

I don't scrub at myself. I dunk my head under once, filling myself up with that submerged rumble, holding my breath, but not for as long as I know I can. I don't want to unnerve Connie. I don't want to make her think I'm trying anything dangerous. When I sit up, the water rushes off me and I hunch over, my head resting on my bent knees, and only when Connie stops speaking do I realize she was talking at all.

I wish for something clear to say, for a cock to crow, for an alarm to sound: anything.

39

I LOOK AROUND for the journal, but don't find it on Julie's nightstand. I get down on the floor to see if it fell beneath the bed. I see a square outlined in light, like what might peek around a trapdoor. I scoot under the bed and my fingers hunt the edges, trying to find a place to pry up the boards to see what's below. I knock, and the space beneath me echoes. I can't find a way to budge the seam of light, though.

"James?" I hear in the room around me. I don't answer. I hear a creak. I think about Connie setting my naked wife on the bed. She must be rifling through our drawers for clean clothes. Maybe she combs Julie's hair. I hear a bird's ritual call from beyond the room, too. The fowl are getting more insistent.

When I was a child, I feared the day I would identify what I wanted to do. What I wanted was to stay free. The worst nightmare appeared to be recognizing how you wanted the world to change.

40

CONNIE CALLS for James. I am used to his disappearing. She walks out to the hall and shouts his name, but he doesn't answer, and I sit on the bed and wait, clear, damp, and heavy, and then something grabs my ankle and I scream and stomp.

It's James's voice I hear call out from beneath the bed, and he emerges, one hand kneading the other, trying to make it feel something other than pain.

"You frightened me," I say, by way of apology.

"Seems like." He wriggles himself free.

I don't ask why he was under the bed, but Connie does. "James, where the hell were you?"

James doesn't answer, and Connie asks where the dirty clothes should go and I point.

"James, you know that Julie has something she's afraid to talk about. She won't tell me, but something has her unglued."

A siren sounds in my mind, and I spring into motion and

shove Connie out of the room and down the hall. She's so surprised that she doesn't resist. She keeps moving down the stairs without my prodding.

"Julie! Stop! What the fuck?"

I follow her, clutching the towel around me, slipping down the last stair, bashing my tailbone, but struggling to stand right away, my body still dripping.

She turns at the crash, finds me on the ground. "Whoa, are you okay?" She pauses.

Even in this moment, she is worried about me, but I reject that worry. I push past her and open the front door and wait for her to go, but she won't cross the threshold so I step outside, nearly naked, so she'll follow me and she does.

"Connie," I shout-whisper, "I didn't ask for that. I need to figure some things out before I start naming this situation, but this is not your responsibility. You think my *husband* doesn't know that something's off?"

Connie throws up her hands. "Get yourself back to the office. Or maybe don't? I don't know that you're the best face to put in front of the board." She stomps down the porch stairs.

"Tell them I'm home for the day," I call.

"Tell them yourself." She slams her car door and takes off.

I walk back inside and lock the door. I gather the strength to deal with James and tug myself upstairs, feeling the ache in my tailbone now. When I pass the guest bedroom, I see a dark shadow and freeze, keeping my eyes on it. "James?"

"*Do* you have something you want to talk to me about?" James asks from the other room. "It seems like you do. I didn't need Connie to tell me that. I was trying to be—"

"James." I stop him. "Could you come here?" The shadow shifts.

"What?" Then he is next to me and I hear him gasp, and I know he is seeing what I see. "What the . . . ," he whispers, afraid, as I am, of something, unsure if we fear scaring the dark spot away or inviting it to stay.

"Hello?" I call into the room but nothing responds. "That's a person's shadow, right?"

"But from where?" he asks.

My heart is rattling and I want to step into the room, but can't bring myself to do it. James steps forward before I get the courage, and as soon as he moves, the shadow disappears, and I look behind him to see if his body is now blocking some light, but the angles don't work that way, and James goes into the room to look for the cause, waving his hand around, trying to figure out what window's light strikes that wall, and he peers outside to see what could have conned our sight. He shakes his head, and when his eyes meet mine, I begin to weep, and he rushes to me and takes me to the bedroom, where we lie down, me still in that damp towel, and I finally breathe normally and hug him until I can't even feel him around me.

41

WHEN JULIE FINALLY drifts off, I duck away to call an electrician, running through the search results until I find one who can pay us a visit today. When he arrives, though, the sound has silenced itself. Without that to point to, I have little to share as a possible symptom of the problem. I describe it. I lead him to the breaker box in the basement. He takes out clamps and gauges. He runs tests. I follow him around as he plugs his equipment into outlets. He tries to pull a clue out of the energy in the walls. When he deems everything in order, he packs his bag. I pay him in cash. I see him out and then I hunt for an answer on my own. I climb stairs. I knock on walls. Still I feel cut out of the equation. *We're a part of this now. Let us in.*

The sun's angle softens. I jostle every room. The moon slides into place. I drive to the bar. I only know the one that Sam has taken me to. Tonight, at least half the seats are filled. This is what *busy* feels like in this town.

I ask any person who sits down what they know about the house. Everyone I talk to has a different story. The bartender ignores me at first, the same way he did the last time I came in. Then he starts to hear what I'm being told. When someone says something he thinks is wrong, he stuffs those gnarled old hands into his pockets until he can break in to correct the person. Each customer is insistent on his own truth.

That the son was an only child.

That there was no son, just the father and the mother and the girl, no brother.

That the sister died and the town ignored it.

That the sister was lost and never found.

That they lived in our house first and then the house next door, and vice versa.

That the girl took care of her brother, and the opposite of that, too.

That they were lovers, not siblings. That they were both at the same time.

"Rolf, then?" I ask. "Was the next-door neighbor, Rolf, involved? He's the brother?"

A woman arrives in a dress too fancy for the bar. Her hair looks as if it would crunch if I touched it. I can't hold her face in my mind. I get the sense I might not recognize her if I saw her again. She drinks her whiskey straight, sipping it rhythmically, like a habit. She is older than me. She possesses the sultry gravity of having arrived in her forties. I remind myself this is all business. Still I slip into the motions of a bar flirt.

"My grandmother talked about the Kinslers," she says. "They went to the same church. Lost one son when he fell out of a tree.

Everyone was happy when they had the daughter, but something was off about her. It's a small town—lots of gossip and stories rumbling about. You know, all friendly 'How do you dos' on Sundays, but the rest of the week, whispers tearing each other down."

"What were they whispering about, though?" I force myself into silence by shoving pretzels in my mouth.

"She had a lot of nervous energy, I guess. Tapped out rhythms, scribbled on any surface she could reach. People wondered why the parents didn't stop her. The mother seemed embarrassed, like nothing could be done, but the father and brother acted like nothing was wrong."

The radius of reason narrows around this woman and me. She is setting out some ground rules I can work with. Her glass is empty. When she goes for her purse, I offer to buy the next round. "Was there something wrong with the girl?"

"That's hard to tell—so much talk was bobbing about and modern medicine wasn't what it is today. I'm sure there was something you could slap a diagnosis on. Hyperactivity, depression, bipolar, schizophrenia, multiple personalities, hysteria, a fugue, aphasia."

My eyes pop at this woman's easy list.

"In the end, I think they decided there was no use in naming her particular brand of dysfunction. My grandmother always used it as an example, especially when they sent me and my sister off to therapy: 'Sometimes there's no righting a wrong.'"

"But they lived in 891, right? Not 895?"

"That is beyond my knowledge," she says. "I can show you where I live, though."

I'm surprised at this suggestion even though, in a different set of circumstances, before I was married, I would have sensed a dynamic growing, too. I might have launched a similar cue. I decline her offer. She smiles wryly. "Such a shame. A new face in town, curious for answers that I might just have."

I thank her for her time. I turn away. I don't want to draw out our farewell any further. The bartender looks at me with pity. He tells me that my companion was making up stories to keep my attention. He points to her sidled up close to a gentleman in a suit near the door. I wonder if the bartender might be right.

The seats around me fill again. No one knows enough.

I make mistakes. I tell people about the sounds we hear. I mention the secret passages. I ask if they know anyone who's had bruises like Julie's. I tell them all the effects hoping they can offer a cause. I ask them if they know about the children in the trees. I meet skeptical glares. They think I'm making it all up. They see me unraveling in front of them.

The room starts to swirl. The bartender tells me that maybe I've had enough. He calls me a cab. I stand outside. I open the door of the first car that pulls up. A blankness takes over.

I wake up on a couch in Rolf's house. I wonder how I got in. I remember only climbing into what I thought was a taxi. My clothes are covered in cat fur. I smell that rank odor. I hear no sounds. I see no lights when I peek up the stairs. I want to flee. Instead, I wait for a while. I tell myself that the shame of asking Rolf how this happened will be mitigated by having an answer. I begin to worry. If Rolf finds me downstairs, he might attack me or call the police. I edge around the corners of the rooms. The kitchen counter is covered in dark, sticky dust.

Dirty dishes pile high blackened by smears of who knows what. I retch at the sour smell. I step out the back door, to try to get away from it. There is no reentering. Rolf surely heard the door slam. He can certainly hear me coughing now. I step down off his back stair. I cross his yard into the woods instead of going home. I hope this decision will save me some guilt. If Rolf sees someone heading into the forest, maybe he won't realize it was me who had let myself in.

I say, "The woods are closer now," and things like that can be true and logical. Forests seed. They grow out. At the beach, the shore appears narrower, too. The trees have advanced in the sand. "The water sneaks up on us," I say. But that's just the tide.

42

I SLEEP THROUGH the afternoon, evening, night. In the morning, I hope James has returned to work, that he left at first light to get an early start, to make up for the time he's missed, but rather than try to figure this out, I slip on shoes and carry myself outside, through the trees, stepping over two that have recently fallen and walk and walk and think about never going home. I hear birds or children calling above me and through the thick trunks, I see someone else within shouting distance. His hair looks like James's but his gait shapes itself the wrong way, and so I stop myself from calling his name. I keep moving until I get to the beach and walk out toward that rocky breakwater. I climb quickly, stumbling as I go, making more work for myself, clutching, feeling how weak my hands are. I scramble over the stone and reach the cave, and as I'm turning to peer inside, Rolf's face rounds the bend to meet mine, lit by a camping lantern in his hand, and his expression is one of surprise, focusing on me as if I might disappear, and I startle and greet him out of impulse, but when I don't dissolve, his wrinkles knit into anger. I see his clothes are soiled and ragged, and he withdraws and his light flips off, but not before I can see that something is written along the back walls. "Turn it back on," I say. I am shaking, unsure I want to step inside, but I do. Rolf moves back into the darkness and it seems clear he knows his way around here and I certainly do not, but I follow him and grab his shoulder, trying to turn him so I can grab hold of the lantern. I expect him to be weak, but he pushes me off and I fall back, skinning my palms, feeling the stone beneath my already tender tailbone. I stand again, still able to see him in the shadow, wondering why he doesn't retreat farther, but I see a glint of light along the ground and realize there's water at the back of the cave. I gather some force and throw a shoulder into his gut and grab the lantern when the blow loosens his grip. With a whimper, higher and weaker than I'd have expected, he crumples against the wall, where puddles dot dimples in the stone, and I feel a jab of contrition for having attacked an old man, but flip the switch and there on the wall are the drawings, like the checkout lady from town told me were hiding in the walls of our house, like James had dreamed: crude figures like the ones in our bedroom, scribbles layered over each other, at different angles like in the journal. "Who did this? Is it you?" I ask.

We are silent together for a long while, but I know what it is to wait when something is coming toward you slowly.

Finally Rolf makes a simple statement: "My sister." I can barely see his eyes beneath the ridge of his brow.

I scan the light slowly past him and can see the writing

extends even to the walls above the water in the back, at least as far as the beam stretches.

I step back to try to see something larger but the lamp doesn't shine far. It shows me some of what I want to know, but leaves out more. The writing brings back the questions of why the journal was in our home, reminds me of the dishware returned to our table through a locked door, my sweater on Rolf's couch.

"Do you come into our house? How do you get in?"

Rolf will not look at me, an irritating reversal of every day preceding this one.

Instead of a response, my ears fill with another sound, like voices in a cathedral, everything echoing, muffled and clear at once. The walls sing in a round. The warm morning has smeared itself on me, has shivered through my jacket until my skin feels spat on under all my layers and the sound is unbearable, like the sound in the house, a rough drone's strata smoothed and compressed like sedimentary rock, and I feel something move through me that amounts to mere nausea and I lean over to vomit at the place where the wall of the cave transforms into the floor, where vertical changes to horizontal, but the man doesn't move toward me. He is uninterested in my weakness.

I feel a knocking despair and pull up my face to see more drips of moisture where the marks run. The smell in the cave loops on itself sharply: urine, moss, mildew.

I shut my eyes tight and reopen them, and the light shines more dimly. I get tired and kneel and try to think clearly, but it's like trying to focus on something caught in your eye, too near the thing to see it. The whine is so loud, I can't hear my own thoughts, and when I look around me, Rolf is gone. I wonder when he left, how long I've been here, and I look toward the back of the cave and wonder if he's waded farther into the darkness, down into the water, if I should dive in and pull him up. I let myself wonder if this is a dream, like the one James had. I make my way out of the cave, into a pink morning light that feels mistaken, and when I emerge, the noise blurs, and the nausea is replaced with a sense of loss.

43

WHEN I REACH our backyard, I can see Julie's car out front and know she hasn't gone to work. I steel myself for the lecture about how worried she was when I didn't come home last night. I hunt for the neighbor in the windows of his house.

At the back door, I see two of my shadow instead of one. I glance behind me to see if I'm being followed. I find no one. I look for something that might be reflecting the sunlight—a cloud or a window—darkening a duplicate of my silhouette on the side of the house. The sky is clear. The windows don't angle themselves the right way. I take a few steps back to see where the shadow gives up. The shadow to my right seems to stutter for a moment. When both shadows fall off the wall, the first lands flat before me on the ground, alone. I notice my breath has formed itself higher in my chest. I let myself inside. In the kitchen, the second shadow returns. This I can make sense of, though. The overhead light is supplemented by the sun through the window. Two light sources allow for two forms on the wall.

I move myself to the bookshelves. I pull off the oversize art books and pile them on the dining room table. I feel the adrenaline relaying up my spine. I sit down to look.

44

ON MY WAY back from the cave, my ankles hinge to push off the unreliable carpet of rotten leaves and my stride flexes to step around rocks and branches.

The woods are quiet and empty. I feel jittery, like the sudden drop of a sugar crash, eager for somewhere soft to stash myself until the feeling passes.

Almost home. Almost home, I repeat to myself. Plucking open the back door feels like crossing a finish line, and I aim for the living room and find James on my way, spread out at the table, circling things in our art books with a red Sharpie. I don't bother to ask what he's up to and I don't inquire as to why he's not at work because it's true that I am also not doing what I'm supposed to do. I sit and pull the couch pillows onto my lap, safe. It feels hard to get words out. "James, I went to the cave." He looks up, the spell of the books broken. "It was like you said, the writing on the walls. Rolf was there until he wasn't, and a sound, too." James looks back down to his work, and I guess that's it. I rest until I get up the energy to search for batteries for the flashlight and James's camera and think about what those walls said, all language that had no apparent order, no logical sentences, no sequences to mine for meaning.

After I gather my supplies, I sit down beside James and look at what he's doing, but none of the circles actually encompasses anything. I flip through the books he's already set aside as finished, but make no sense of them. I turn to him and grab the hand with the marker. "James, you're ruining them."

He says nothing, pulls his hand away to lean his marker against the page, and finally I can see. It's the shadows he's circling.

45

"JAMES, THIS ISN'T helping. This isn't all a trick of the light. I don't think you're going to figure it out by studying photographs." Julie tucks my hair behind my ear and places a hand on my leg, watching me, and I feel her familiar tenderness and finally turn to her.

She tells me about the cave. Her voice is soft and matter-of-fact. I tell her about the haze of particulars I found on that barstool. Everything points to Rolf's being connected to this house. Despite how far apart we are at the moment, Julie and I can feel that tiny overlap in our Venn diagram. That connection allows a little bit of the problem to disappear.

Julie idly massages my hand while she talks. She rubs tiny circles into the fleshy base of my palm and then squeezes each finger in three different spots, pulling gently on the end of each. She looks over my shoulder to remember and then into my eyes for confirmation. Julie brings up some specific drawing she saw in the cave. That image is nowhere to be found in my memory of my time there. She goes on. It sounds familiar now. I get overly sure. Julie tells me something she read on the wall. I feel convinced I remember that, too, but then uncertain. I worry I'm creating false memories. I consider whether I can call that experience. "This all sounds right, but now I'm questioning myself. I heard that if you remember a thing, you corrupt it. If you want to remember something closest to its truth, the trick is to remember it rarely. But, of course, if you don't remember a thing often enough, you're bound to forget it. There is no way for memory to be pure." This is the closest I've felt to her in a long time. Everything is laid out between us. Julie is insistent on solving the mystery. I keep trying to talk myself out of believing there is a mystery at all.

Julie says, "I don't know how you knew about the cave, but you were right." She still can't believe that I was really there. I wince. I grip her hand more tightly. I hold on. Julie tells me a game plan. We'll return to the cave with brighter lights. I'll take photos so we have something solid to reference.

I feel this threat to our credibility sharply behind my eyes. The inability to trust ourselves is the most menacing danger. I fear what we could find there. I fear what we won't.

What is worse? To be confronted with an obvious horror, or to be haunted by a never-ending premonition of what's ahead?

46

I WANT TO return to the cave immediately, but James sees the scrapes on my palms, the new bruises on my knees and forearms from my climb up the rocks, my struggle with Rolf, and insists we wait until I've healed.

I ask where James put the journal, but he says it's disappeared. I tap around the passage that had opened in the bedroom to see if it will open again, if the book has been returned to where I found it, with no luck. I wonder if Rolf has come into our home again. I wonder if James is hiding the book from me, hoarding some knowledge he's gathering from it or preventing me from feeding my obsession.

I watch the neighbor's house, looking for him in the windows and not finding him, wondering if he's still back somewhere in the cave. I try to convince James to return with me. I tell the office I need to work from home around some repairs. I'm supposed to be doing research for a new product anyway. I tell my boss the timing is perfect. I'll be able to focus without interruption and come in later in the week with a preliminary project plan. I expect an angry email from Connie, but hear nothing.

On the third day, still with no sign of him, I ring Rolf's doorbell. I want to ask him more about the cave and our house. I worry something might have happened, that I could have caused a panic in him, but there's my imagination again, prying itself open, sketching itself out. I think about opening the door and letting myself in. I tell myself that just because I've already done something doesn't make it okay to do it again.

I sit at the window, and James asks me what I'm doing and I say, "Waiting."

"You know you've turned into him, right? Watching for him the way he looked for us? What if he's in the house and not answering?"

"No light ever comes on."

James says, "Maybe you've finally run him off."

"That is really the last thing I want." I mean it.

"I appreciate your attempts to solve this case, Nancy Drew, but maybe we should mind our own business."

But I keep my eyes trained out the window.

47

I LOOK AT job openings. Every posting says "Experience required." I fixate on that threshold. An hour, a day, a year?

Every day I get a call from the office asking where I am. On the fifth day, my boss apologizes for relaying the information via voice mail. I've been terminated. "Good riddance," I sigh. I delete the message.

Julie doesn't notice. In all of the distraction, she sees me leave the house every day and return home. She doesn't question my destination. She doesn't realize I've been going to the library. I tell myself I'm looking for work. Really, I spend more time hunting for clues to our puzzle. I hunt the microfiche for more information about Rolf's family and the history of our house. Nothing is coming together, though. I scoot the computer screen right up to the edge of the desk to get a better look. I push my eyes as close as possible so I can see the grid of pixels. I can't see the graininess I used to with older screens. I miss that shocking fluorescence that would appear if you got in tight enough.

I call Sam to ask him if he has any job leads. He whispers, "Jim, I don't think you should be calling me here anymore. I can talk to you later from home. Deal?"

"Do you want to get a beer tonight?" I ask.

"I think it's better if we don't." He hangs up. I can't blame him.

I'd had no interest in walking into a boss's office and quitting. I thought I would see how much they'd put up with before I was let go. I was taking chances and hoping for the worst. I was hoping the worst would hold out for as long as possible.

That night, Julie and I play Battleship with our laptops—that's what we call it when we sit across the table from one another with our screens open. I let myself hunt job listings inches away from her. I have grown bold. We've been quiet for so long that when she says my name suddenly, I startle.

I close my browser instinctively. I look up. She's staring not at me, but past me. I realize she might have seen the reflection of my screen in the glass of the china cabinet. "What?" I already feel sick at having to talk through this with her.

Her eyes are not on the cabinet, though, but lower. I turn to look. She whispers, "In the kitchen." I look at the crack of light under the closed door. Divided into threes, a shadow the width and placement of what one might assume are two feet breaks up the line of light.

I train my eyes on it. I cycle through answers in my mind. Nothing makes sense. I hold out my hand to indicate she shouldn't move. I grab the fireplace poker. I try to approach the door quietly. A floorboard creaks. I watch the shadow shuffle slightly. "Hello?" I call.

I push the door open.

There is nothing at all on the other side: just the kitchen in the yellow glow of the light above the stove. I look into the pantry. I look down the basement stairs. My sight returns nothing.

In the dining room, I close the door to the kitchen again. We inspect the crack of light for the shadow. It's seamless now. Once we've confirmed this, I prop open the door. "Why was this closed anyway?" I ask.

"I didn't want the heat of the oven to get the whole house hot."

I take another lap around. I look in every hiding spot we know of. I punch into the free ceiling tile in the basement. I peer behind the loose brick in the fireplace. I inspect the guest room carefully. We appear to be alone.

48

AT NIGHT, I try to sleep, but can't. I sit by the window, looking for that missing gaze. James says, "Lie down. I'll tell you a bedtime story," and he does, but the story lacks a proper ending.

"Does the man get over the wall?" I ask, but he doesn't know. "Does the dog live?" He doesn't know that either.

"I see some barbed wire or chicken wire or something," he says, as if the story is coming to him in a vision.

"Make up the ending."

He says it's not that simple.

I run my feet along the cool sheets at the bottom of the bed and feel something grainy. "What's all that grime down there? Are your feet dirty?"

James says he went to the beach, that he forgets about the spaces between his toes, that more sand is always hiding there.

"Well, go rinse it off." But he doesn't move. "James, I just changed these sheets. Will you go rinse off your feet?" But he's already asleep, as if nothing I say could even matter all that much. I lie in bed unable to quiet my mind.

In the story, a man is trying to escape a prison, not a government prison, but more like he's held captive by a villain and he sees an opportunity to get free, but he's grown attached to this dog who's in the yard where he is being held and he wants the dog to be free, too. He's pulled loose some of the barbed wire lining the top of the fence and thinks he might be able to scramble over the cement wall if he can get enough momentum, but not while holding the dog, so he ties a rope around the dog as a harness, and he ties that rope to his belt and he scrambles up to the top of the fence and starts to haul up the dog, but the dog is frantic, and not interested in being airborne, and the man knows that if he lifts that dog, it will whine and bark, and the villain might emerge at the ruckus and shoot the man or drag him back down into the yard and kill or torture both of them. But the man cannot decide what to do: free himself or take a risk.

After James falls asleep, I decide I should call the police. I tell myself I should wait until morning, but once I've made my decision, I need to act.

I slip out of bed and into the guest room. I hunt the walls for shadows I don't want to see. I dial the nonemergency number. "I'd like to report a missing person."

49

I FIND JULIE sitting under a blanket on the front porch. I join her. We are quiet for a long time. We see the lights of the police cars pull up.

We watch them knock on the neighbor's door. There is no answer. They let themselves in. They stay inside for a long time. More arrive. We get up the courage to go talk to them.

"You're the one who called us?" an officer with a deep scar down his cheek asks Julie. There isn't an iota of blame in his voice.

"Yes, I'm Julie." She shakes his hand.

The officer lifts his eyes over Julie to me. "You're another neighbor?"

"I'm Julie's husband." I try to stay friendly. I hold out my hand. "James Khoury." The officer doesn't break eye contact. I never know if I'm supposed to do the same or look away. Which is more confrontational? Is this a moment to abide or resist?

"When was the last time you saw him?" the officer asks.

Julie pauses. She feels guilty, but not of a crime. "Friday. I saw him Friday by the beach."

"He seemed well?" the officer asks.

"I think so. As well as well was for him. Obviously, he's old."

"And it's unusual that you wouldn't have seen him for as many days as this?"

"I thought he was homebound before I saw him the other day." She pauses, then absently adds, "He watches us. From his windows, and he hasn't been watching lately."

The cop lifts an eyebrow. The situation shifts. "If we don't find anything inside, we'll search the woods and the lake, too. We'll locate him."

The cop looks back at the house, now a blaze of light. We see men appearing in the windows, rooms we've never viewed before, dulled by the layers of curtains: dioramas thinly veiled. It's impossible not to think of our own home. Its bare glass showcases everything we do.

The labor of this night wells up in us. Julie thanks the officer. "We're going to head back inside, but please let us know if there's anything you need."

"Will do, ma'am." The officer tips his chin at me.

We climb our stairs. We step through the front door. We hide behind a wall that is more keeping us in than keeping anything out.

50

"YOU CALLED THE police?" I ask Julie. "I wish you'd talked to me about it first."

"You would have stopped me." Her mouth forms a loose grin she can't help. It shape-shifts into apology.

I deny this. "Maybe. I'd like to be involved, though. How will we go back to the cave now that a bunch of police are swarming the area?"

Julie's face flashes between regret and indifference. "We can still hike up there. Maybe the police can tell us more about what's going on in the cave. They must know about it already, or if not, they should. Maybe this will help us make some progress."

"You think they're going to share what they find with us? You have a lot more trust in law enforcement than I do, I guess."

Julie winces. She has never had a run-in with the law. She has never been targeted because of her looks. She has never felt betrayed by a lack of action. To her, calling the police is the right thing to do. She doesn't question it.

I hug her. I apologize. This is the Julie I love. She tries to solve every issue immediately. She calls her clients to tell them the problem will be fixed before they even know it exists. She is always a step ahead. I know waiting even this long to call the police or to return to the cave herself has required a gargantuan patience of her.

"But you'd like some answers, too, right? That's what you said. It's not just me?"

"Yes," I admit. "But I don't know if I can trust the answers coming from someone else. I want to find our own."

"And if that's not possible?"

"Then maybe I can live with the questions."

51

THE POLICE GIVE some of Rolf's bedsheets to a hound. It turns up nothing. A day later, a neighborhood dog returns home with the last two joints of a pinkie. The dog's owners call the police. The process starts again. The hound hunts through the woods. It finds a patch of matted blood and protein left behind in a hollowed tree trunk, covered in insects. The police set up lights inside the tree to photograph the clump of evidence. They move carefully around the area looking for clues. If it were a case of Rolf's having been disoriented or drunk, they'd have found him by now. If he'd been attacked by a dog or another animal, they'd have found him. They would have found him in his house or at a hospital or sprawled somewhere in the woods. All they find, though, are these meager traces.

We knock on the window of the car and the plainclothes detectives who never leave our street now listen to our questions. "Seems like Mr. Kinsler doesn't want us to find him," they say.

We ask them if they need anything: drinks or snacks or a clean bathroom.

The police think in pictures. They think of guns and rope and wire and knives. None of this can be determined with so little evidence. They reenter the man's home. It presents a smell and suggestion of its own. This man had worked his way to the bottom of his quality of living: a slump.

52

I SIT SOLID, hands in my lap, head down, as the sorrow wraps itself tighter around me. If they find Rolf, it won't be a solution so much as a red herring. The questions we ask are breeding. It's hard to focus on just one. My hope dips again. My mood sketches itself on the wall in primitive, toothy grins, as James tries to draw me out of myself, but I am reluctant to go. I am accustomed to being prepared and solving problems. I am starting to think this mess will not transform into memory. I feel envy for people with ordinary lives. My analytical mind ties itself in knots trying to reason through our situation, almost as if trying to understand what's happening is making it worse.

I hear something below James and me, something like a thump and a creak. A muffled thud and then the slide of metal against metal. "Did you hear that?"

James pours cereal into a bowl. "This?"

"No, something downstairs, like furniture being moved or a hinge flexing."

"Do you want me to take a look?"

I don't want him to put himself in danger, but I want to know. "Yes."

I listen to him open the door to the basement and head down the stairs. I brace myself for the sounds of a struggle or a scream. I hear another creak and then his footsteps are climbing again. The door to the basement closes and James enters the room. "I think that metal cabinet down there needs a new handle and maybe a new shelf. The door was open and some of the stuff had fallen out. I put it back, but the door doesn't properly close. I'm not sure it will hold."

I can't help but think about *The Lion, the Witch and the Wardrobe*. I want to ask if James checked to see what was behind the cabinet, but I stop myself. "Stuff fell out of the cabinet on its own." I don't add a question mark to the sentence. I speak it like a fact. I try it out.

"Weirder things have happened." James spoons cereal into his mouth.

"And they do, all around us, every day it seems." I look into James's cereal bowl, almost empty, all milk until a piece of wheat surfaces from nowhere and James captures it with his spoon and fits it into his still-full mouth.

"Julie, do you want to move?"

That is not a question I am expecting and I feel myself start to speak, but I am still on the ground and I would need to drift above myself to get the words out.

There are times when saying nothing means nothing, and then there are times when nothing holds an answer. Pathetic distractions pull James away from me, and he thinks my silence is without substance, but I think it means the world.

This house is sapping us, pulling out our cores. Our filthy roots expose themselves, but our faces are clean and wide. "Maybe we could stay somewhere else for a little while. Even a night or two," I say. I am reluctant to give up my vigil. Staying seems like self-inflicted distress, but I also don't believe I'd be able to leave for good. With all the financial gymnastics we'd have to perform, favors to ask, possible habits that could re-awaken, the defeat of it feels larger than the threats we face if we stay. I know the bulk of the work will fall on me. I stare at the middle distance between those points.

James says, "Tell me when and where."

Normally I flare at having a task to tackle, but today I wear down. I sag. I sully.

53

THE DETECTIVES KNOCK on *our* door this time. Some new questions have come up around Rolf's disappearance. The minutes feel smooth when they are out of our control.

The officers settle themselves. Julie brings us all cups of coffee. "I'm so sorry," I say. "I don't remember your names."

"O'Neill and Poremski," the taller detective says pointing first to himself and then his partner. He's the only one who ever talks. "How well do you know Rolf Kinsler?"

I've told Julie not to say too much. Risk wraps all of our stories.

Julie says, "Not very well. We introduced ourselves when we first moved in. He wasn't interested in getting to know us, but I had a dream about him last night, that he was growing extra fingers, first on his hands, but when the palms and backs of his hands were covered, they started growing up his arms, until he looked like some kind of anemone."

I take her hand. "Julie, stick to the questions." I hope to call up the Julie that knows better from deep inside her.

"Do you have an idea of what this dream might mean, Mrs. Khoury?"

"Are you a dream interpreter, Detective?" I ask.

"Might be. Depends on what her answer is." He sneers at me. I can tell he's not impressed with what I think I know.

"We're not going to find him," she says frankly.

"What makes you say that?"

"That man had loads of secrets, more than we'll be able to figure out, but I'm curious what else *you* can tell *us* about *him*," my wife says, artfully trying to turn the tables, to test whether this exchange is as one-sided as I predicted it would be.

"With all due respect, ma'am, we'll ask the questions."

"Can you tell us more once his body is found?" I ask.

"Why are you so sure he's dead?" the detective asks.

"I assume. We know he was seriously injured because of what you found in the woods. He hasn't been located. With that much blood, how could he survive?"

"It's incredible what the body is capable of, so we're not calling his life lost quite yet. Tell me, Mrs. Khoury, I'm told that you said something about him watching you to one of the officers. Can you tell us more about that?"

Julie glances at me looking for approval. I pretend that she is pausing before she decides how to respond. I don't react. The officer notices, though. I'm sure they're convinced I'm responsible for something and I'm forcing Julie to help me cover it up.

"You can be honest with us, Mrs. Khoury. You don't have to ask your husband's permission." He says the word *husband* in a way that implies I'm nothing of the sort, but instead a trickster or a con artist using her for who knows what.

"We were suspicious of him. He was nosy in a far-off kind of way," she says. "Often when we were getting home, I would see his face staring at us from behind his window, and I can't say we welcomed that."

"How did you respond?"

"Honestly, I stared back hoping he would stop, but it rarely worked."

"Mr. Khoury, did you also see Mr. Kinsler spying on you?"

"Not as much as Julie. She would call me over to look. He often disappeared before I made it to the window." While this answer is true, I regret making a comment that would call Julie into question.

"And can you think of anything you were doing that might have made Mr. Kinsler suspicious of you? Like he had to keep an eye on you for his own safety?"

I fear she might tell them about the way we dug around the yard looking for bodies. I worry she'll reveal all the objects I pulled inside out. I'm concerned she might say that the man knew something about the house. He might have had answers about why it was so strange and full of folds. He might have been waiting to watch us get driven out. I jump in before Julie can answer. "I don't think so, Detective. We're pretty boring people. Tried to be friendly. He wasn't having it."

"But you didn't go over there and ask him to leave your wife alone?"

I stay calm. I try to ignore the insult to my masculinity. "Now that you ask, yes. I did go knock on his door. He didn't answer."

"And when did you say you last saw him?"

"Friday," Julie answers.

They look to each other to see if either has anything else to ask. "Okay, that's it for now. If you think of any additional information, please contact us right away." The detectives rise and head to the entryway. As we shut the door behind them, Julie tells me her stomach is cramping up. I lean her into me. I kiss her cheek. I tell her we're alone now as if it were a comfort.

54

I ARRIVE AT the doctor's and strip down and slip into a gown the consistency of a cheap bedsheet washed too many times and I crinkle up onto the paper-covered examination table. After a night of no sleep, crimped with sharp intervals of pain, I woke early to see if the office had an opening.

The doctor tells me to lie back and begins pressing on my abdomen and I recoil, and she says, "That hurts?" I say it does, trying not to be a wimp about it. "What about here?" She presses on the other side, but again, the pain flips itself through me, and my legs curl to block her. "Okay, sorry for any discomfort. I'll let you relax for a second. Why don't you sit up, and I'll do the rest of the exam?" She looks in my eyes, ears, nose, and down my throat, and she tests my reflexes and my muscle strength. "Let's try the pelvic exam again," she says, trying to sound as confident as she can, and I agree because I don't know what else to do. "Your reaction leads me to believe there could be some sort of infection, so I'll go slowly and we'll try to figure out what the trouble is, okay, Julie? Was anything bothering you before you phoned?" She has an ease and natural beauty that makes me wonder why anyone wears makeup or colors her hair, why everyone doesn't covet a motherly belly showcased in high-waisted pants.

"Last night, I started to have some cramping, but I assumed it was because I've been under a lot of stress."

"Okay." She angles in the speculum and she is gentle and the pain is less severe and she shines a light inside and says, "Okay, well, it does appear that your cervix is bruised. Have you had any trauma in that region recently? Vigorous activity?" She raises her eyebrows, matter-of-fact.

I tell her no. I flash to falling on the stairs and then in the cave, but it doesn't seem as if the impact could have rippled so deep.

"I think we'll perform an ultrasound then, so we can figure out what's causing this. Stay here, and we'll get everything set up."

I feel as if I should be worried, as if I should get my priorities straight and fear for my life, but I feel numb, sure now that I know where this internal bruise has come from, like all the others: it's that house that's been sinking into me, farther and farther. I want to suggest this, but I want her to give me another answer.

A nurse arrives and keeps a hand clamped on the back of my gown as she accompanies me to the next room.

As I lie on the table, they rub the jelly onto my pelvis and examine the screen and zoom in and point to different areas. I look away and notice how delicate the doctor's ankles are in her kitten-heel pumps. I look up when she tells me they see a cyst that's burst. The blood broken free of its vessels has spread and they tell me it might have happened this morning, and that the tenderness will clear up in a couple of days and they give me a prescription for pain medication to take sparingly as needed.

The doctor says they'll be doing some tests to determine the cause of the cyst and the severity. "We can do a full blood workup for you in the next few days. Is there someone I can call to take you home?"

I think carefully and give them Connie's number.

55

"MY GOD," I say when I find Julie at home, in bed. "Why didn't you call me?"

"There was no rush. You'd get home eventually."

I fume inside. It's not the right response, though. I know that. "What can I get you?"

She is already falling asleep again.

I make a thermos of tea. I fill her water glass. I place these next to the bed beside the bottle of pain medication. I watch her for a while. I go downstairs. I scan through channels. I turn the TV off. I pull on my boots and head out the back door. There is no opening between the trees at the back of the yard tonight. I bend a few around me. They swerve as if they were made of gum and rubber. They don't fall. The forest's density feels more like a jungle now. I shove and form doorways for myself. I wonder where the chirps are coming from. It doesn't seem as if there could be room enough for birds. Their vacant, avian bones shouldn't be strong enough to form space in the tight weave of branches.

When the beach is in my sight, I feel a shove. I fall forward onto the sand. The trees have pushed me out. They've pulled themselves back together again. I peer into the water. The ripples show eyes staring back up at me. When I focus, the vision is gone.

I think, *You should be there if she needs you.* I think, *This is selfish. Turn around. Your wife is in pain. You are running from it.* I fixate on the pus and tissue that layered itself inside her. I feel my breath start to leave me. I try to think of something else. The feed of my thoughts, though, has been jump-started. I recognize the bright terror coursing through me. Every minute renders me closer to pitch-darkness. I want to break the seal into the next day. I want to forget what is happening now. I know it isn't that easy. I want to believe time has already passed. I want to reason my way through it. I am overcome. The tide is fast approaching.

I let it have me. The brackish water reaches over me. Under the waves, without my breath, I find a tinted version of myself.

I can't tell where my skin stops. I can't tell where the night begins. I gasp for air. I cannot find it.

56

THE PAIN HAS gotten worse, but the doctor warned of this. I hoist myself out of bed to look for James. The wallpaper of the hallway undulates with a pattern I don't remember and the floor pulses quietly beneath my feet and the air frays with blips at a frequency I can't hear, but I tell myself that is just my head pounding. I trick open my robe to let some air in and feel suddenly warm and endangered and consider lying down in the hallway, but push forward.

I take one stair at a time, regarding the banister with expectation, waiting for everything to start reacting: any second, this world will come alive like some *Fantasia* playing out in my mind. I arrive at new instincts: to skip the last three stairs and jump down, to touch every door handle as if there might be a fire on the other side. I head toward the picture window, looking out at the backyard, and what I see diffuses my boldness. The trees have stretched over the lawn, nearer, almost to the back door, throbbing forward and back, and beyond that, even through the density of the forest, I can see the water struggling wide and tall through the trunks, closer than it's ever been, and all those cranky birds silence themselves, and I should be afraid, but I am so happy at the prospect of being washed away.

I take a deep breath and I swear I can feel my blood pick up oxygen and carry it through me, delivering questions that blink rapidly behind my eyes like closed captions.

I settle my body onto the cool linoleum and wait.

57

ROLLING IN THE tide's lace, I sputter awake. I cough up sand and burning water. I trek home, soaked through.

Inside the back door, Julie breathes deeply on the floor. I think, *Again?* Patterns are developing.

I wake her. I expect her to be disoriented. She isn't. She grabs my arm to stand. She feels my wet sleeve. "Where were you?"

I skip the response. "Can you make it upstairs? I can carry you."

"No, no. I can manage." She moves slowly, off-kilter. She recovers from having woken up on the floor. She uses one hand to pull the other wrist over her head and then swaps sides. At the stairs, she lets out a yawn loud enough to sound like a cry. "That felt good."

I follow close behind her. I am ready to catch her if she loses her balance. She turns at the top of the stairs. She doesn't flip the light on in our room. I don't either. I drop my wet clothes in a pile below the drawings on the wall. I join her.

"Talk to me."

She does. We are both so tired and messy. Our brains have become disorganized with exhaustion.

"The woods, are they still so close?" she asks. I am confused. "Look out the window."

I pull myself up in bed. I gaze out the back window. There is nothing to find. "Tell me more."

"When I woke up, the forest was marching closer to the house, and the water was coming through the trees and it all felt unreal."

"The waves were big tonight, but not that big, Julie." I wait for her to ask me why I am wet. I wait for her to inquire about my well-being. I lie down again. I pull Julie to me. I hope to transfer the questions I want to be asked into her. I hope they permeate from my open pores into hers.

58

WE DOZE POORLY, and when we rouse ourselves, it feels like something else. Without the comparison to sleep, waking doesn't feel like much at all.

I still feel tender, but I head downstairs to make breakfast: eggs and bacon and hash browns. James emerges to the smells and we eat as if we've gone without for days. I feel bolstered, as if I want to take something on. A plan forms quickly in my head and I pose it for James. "I want to return to the cave. Now. I feel good. I want to take the pictures of the walls."

James is skeptical, but he doesn't fight me. I dress with urgency, wincing as I lift my arms to put on a shirt, and I realize I need to hide my pain from James or he will force me to stay put.

The air is wet with summer humidity, and the ground gives soggily beneath our feet. I look at James as if to say, *See? The waves reached this far.* My feet work hard to lift themselves up from the soft mud, and I feel a sharp pain in my hips each time I pivot forward, but I continue.

"Are you sure you're well enough to do this?"

"I'll be fine," I say, determined and wanting to be done already.

After we've undergone the trial of working our way through the mud, the sand shapes itself into a mold for our strides. We quicken as we approach the rocky hill, and then the beach leads into the solid boulders. The anticipation of reaching the cave has won out, and I no longer register the pain pulsing through my belly. I have trouble finding a root or rock to clutch and haul myself up the final stretch, but I grip the rough stone and push off with my right leg and raise the left as high as I can to reach the ground in front of the cave. I stand and breathe for a moment as James completes his ascent close behind me, and when I look inside, the ache returns to my gut, racking through.

59

NOTHING. NOT WHAT I remember from my dream. Not what Julie saw when she found the neighbor here. We make our way to the back of the cave. The walls gape and drip. Blank. A clog in our sight.

Julie asks, "Where could all of that writing have gone?"

In the pauses, I stifle my worries. *Maybe I did only dream what I saw. Maybe Julie's mind made up a truth to affirm what I'd told her. Maybe she turned abstract shadows on the wall into some sort of language. Something imaginary can stick. Something false can feel real.*

"The waves," Julie says, "they must have washed it all away."

I feel these words like a rusty wire through my veins. They rascal through. I know this impression of turning over inside myself. I know how it feels to speak a lie to make it sound more true.

60

WHEN I RETURN to work, Connie takes me to lunch. I fill her in. I have an idea of how she can help us, and I am prepared to ask for it.

I tell her everything she needs to know, sidestepping the most extreme parts, but touching on the basics: the cave, the missing neighbor, the police. "I mean, I know what this looks like. If it wasn't clear before, I've certainly lost it now, right?"

"I think you're a strong lady. I mean, I ran away when I thought you were being stubborn, and look at all you stick around for. You're putting up with a lot of weird-ass shit."

I exhale. "I know. But I can't run because at least some of it *is* me. I have to admit that, but I'm starting to doubt myself. Is the house haunted? Or am I imagining things? Am I trying to manufacture some sort of tipping point so we can leave?"

"I don't know, but you and James are welcome to come stay with me. Anytime. Come take a break and see how things go."

This invitation sends an optimistic buzz through me; she has offered without my having to ask. "Really? We might take you up on that. I would love to feel normal again."

"The perils of being a homeowner, huh?"

"My God, is that all it is?" I drain my beer.

"A second?"

I cock my head as if it were the most obvious thing in the world.

Connie laughs. "I believe you, Julie. I didn't want to, but I do."

That's really the most I could ask from anyone: to hear someone say that I count more in her mind than logic. But I need to force myself out of thinking this is something so extraordinary that it merits that sort of attention. I roll my eyes. "Don't let me take you down with me."

61

I STOP AT the grocery store that night, and the checkout lady recognizes me. "That neighbor of yers is off missin', huh?"

I swallow hard, a hockey puck through a drinking straw. "I guess so." I try to force worry and sympathy into my voice. I have lost track of my concern for Rolf and turned it on myself.

"Must be Alz-hammers." Her eyebrows are drawn on at a slant today, stopping short of curving down in the middle, so she has an expression of concern even though the rest of her face remains blank. "Shame that someone wasn't takin' care of him. Now he's gone and got himself lost."

I inhale, afraid to say more.

"Did he seem confused to yah?" She scans the bagels, coffee, frozen fish fillets, and glances up at me.

I allow my head the slimmest pivot right, then left.

"That's how they say it goes: all there one minute, vanished

in the maze of yer mind the next. It's hard to understand it, but I guess that's the point."

"If the point is that it's pointless," I mumble, and slide my card.

She frowns and looks away. "Well, anyway, nice to see yah. I'll say a prayer for yer neighbor. Take care now."

I thank her and drive the dark road home, the canopy of trees having grown so dense with the summer rain it's like driving through a tunnel. I allow myself to consider the possibility that Rolf had lost control of his mind before he lost himself to the woods or the water or wherever he might be. Even if this was true, I could still see a logic to his world, enough of a story that I could almost grab hold of it and imagine what filled the gaps.

Coming in the front door, I eye the photo of my stepmother as a little girl on the wall and then another of my step-grandmother as a teen right next to it, stained, blotched bright, as if the light is in the viewer's eyes, like when you look at a person haloed against the sun and you can only see their faulty edges burned away by the shine.

When her mother died, I helped Carol clean out the house and found these photos in a box. I asked her if I could have them. "Sure," she said. "They're all muddled with water damage and fading. What would I do with them?"

"I'll take them, then." I tried not to feel judged.

I stand and watch as that stain shifts around the grand-mother I have no claim to, her chin and left cheek disappearing to the burst, then surfacing again, the blemish hiding her other half.

"James, how can a stain move around a picture?"

He tilts his head.

"James, Connie offered for us to stay with her for a while to get away from here and see how we feel."

James approaches the idea carefully. I watch him roll it around. "Yes," he says. "Let's try it."

62

"PLEASE, PLEASE. Come in!" Connie wraps her arms around Julie. When they let go, there's a moment of hesitation. Connie and I half hug. I inhale a few of her curls, but don't acknowledge it. We release quickly. "I put new sheets on the bed in the guest room for you. You can have the bathroom next to it all to yourselves. Anything in the fridge? Yours! Don't fuck up my DVR, though, okay? Welcome!"

We laugh. Connie invites us into the kitchen. She's set out bagels, muffins, and fresh coffee. "Jeez, Connie, you're not hosting a B and B here. You didn't need to go to any trouble. This is too much."

"It's no trouble at all. I'll be right back!" She disappears upstairs.

"This is really nice of her," I say to Julie. "I was convinced she hated me. I wasn't expecting this."

Julie looks at me a little bewildered. "Me neither. And

she doesn't hate you; it's just that she can't see the full picture. She's protective of me."

I try not to feel defensive. "This blueberry muffin is mine." I pour myself a cup of coffee.

Connie returns. "So, what's on the docket? Should we sit on the back porch? It's a beautiful day!"

"You don't need to entertain us, Connie. I'm just going to read my book," I say.

"*Fine.* Miss out on all the fun. What do you think, Julie: patio?" I notice the way the tip of Connie's nose moves, ever so slightly, as she talks. When she closes her mouth, her nose pulls down a bit, like a bunny, sniffing.

Julie smiles sheepishly. "I know it's early, but I could use a drink."

"Eleven a.m. is five o'clock somewhere! You're my kind of lady." Connie stands up from her chair and goes to the corner cabinet. She pulls out a bottle of tequila. "How about some agua fresca? I have fresh watermelon in the fridge."

The offer is too good to pass up. "I'm in," I say.

Connie pours me a drink and I carry my book outside to read. I fail. Julie and Connie take over the silence with layer on layer of jokes and gossip.

They argue about some elaborate card trick they remember from a television special they watched in their dorm room. Connie produces a deck of cards. Her attempt at the trick fails again and again. I'm convinced I can pull it off. I can't. Nothing has ever been funnier. We shift to several hands of gin rummy. Then we play a round of a more violent game I've never heard of. I never quite wrap my mind around the rules. Connie wins.

When we look up, the sun is already descending into a pink smear at the tree line.

"How are we at the end of this day already?" Julie asks. It has been so long since time has passed quickly and easily.

We decide to walk the mile to dinner. We'll sober up while we stroll. We'll fill ourselves with tacos for the walk home. "Are there actually sidewalks all the way there?" I ask.

"Yes. This place is in that strip mall with the urgent-care clinic and the bakery. I walked over there this morning actually."

Julie and I disappear to change our clothes. Julie slips on a dress amplified by a floral print. "How do I look?"

"Like a svelte garden," I say. I know she'll like that.

"How do you feel?"

"Mostly, I feel those drinks. They feel terrific. You?"

"Yes, it seems right to be away from that place."

"So let's sell it," I say, as if it were an easy thing to do. "Let's rent an apartment and get out of there until someone wants to take it off our hands."

"Don't you think we got such a good deal on it because it's a hard house to sell? The bank owned it for years."

"So, let's make it our project. We'll fix it up. Install new plaster in the basement to get rid of that stain. Replace all those old windows. We could put new cabinets in the kitchen. We probably need to stay in the house while we do it, but it'll be over quickly. We'll be free."

"You make it sound so simple, James, but I really don't think it is."

"Maybe we can make it easy. Maybe we're part of the problem. Maybe we're letting ourselves believe it's out of our control."

"If that's the case, then we should stay and stop being so paranoid." Julie is always reading into what I say.

"No, we know we want to get rid of the house. Let's do it. Maybe we can try to think more rationally if the situation is temporary, though. We don't have to let it get to us."

Julie looks skeptical and then notices I am still in my T-shirt and shorts. "Aren't you changing?"

"Yes." I jump up. I pull my shirt out of my bag.

"Ready, ladies?" Connie calls from outside the door.

"Uno momento por favor!" I shout.

Julie grabs her purse. She squeezes out. "What's this place called?" I hear her ask Connie.

"Mataviejitas. That's what they call their margarita."

Julie laughs.

I emerge. "Mataviejitas? Accessing my high school Spanish . . . *beep boop bop* . . . Old Lady Killer? Is that right?"

I catch the grimace on Connie's face as I start down the stairs.

"I think so. Too grim? At least it's not Old Man Killer."

Julie winces.

Connie asks, "Do you want to go somewhere else? There's a bar in the other direction that serves tapas."

"Don't be silly. I'd like to take my old ladies to meet their maker. How do I look?" At the bottom of the stairs, I do a sloppy spin. I catch myself on the banister.

Connie's eyes go wide. "Very smooth. Maybe you skip the next round, pal."

I bow deeply.

Julie rubs my back. "You look very handsome, James. You could have given your hair a comb, but this is definitely an improvement."

"I can brush my hair! I'll be back down in two shakes. Why don't you ladies get a head start? I'll catch up."

Julie shoots me a look. She feels guilty for having made this request. She's not stopping me, though.

When I appear at the front door a minute later, they've only made it to the sidewalk. Connie says, "Let's skedaddle. I don't want to have to wait for a table."

"Connie, don't I need to lock this?" I ask.

"Nah, I don't usually."

"Live dangerously," I say. Connie's Christmas tree lies on the parkway waiting to be picked up. "Trash service is no good over here, huh?"

"Friends, that had clearly been in my house for over five months, and I would like to thank you both for staying here because otherwise it would have stuck around until next Christmas."

We walk along a park dense with trees. We can see through to a clearing with a huge playground. No children play on the slides, swings, monkey bars. A couple of mothers with strollers are planted beneath a huge tree. They stare up. "Come down now," one calls. Whatever is in that tree doesn't respond.

"Wait up, ladies!" I shout. I jog ahead. I squeeze both their shoulders.

"Ah!" Julie grunts. Her hand goes to her neck.

"Come on, I didn't grab it that hard!"

She pulls back the corner of her sweater. The edge of another bruise is already feathering into view.

63

AT THE END of the meal, Connie insists on examining the new bruise, asks me to summarize the latest results from the doctors, which amount to not much insight at all, and then counters, "I think you should get a second opinion."

"I know and I will." I reach over to clasp James's hand for a moment before excusing myself to go to the bathroom.

I still feel followed, as if instead of the house's being haunted, the haunting has crawled into me, and I want to turn the tale as James had said, so that I believe both that we are lucky and that nothing matters, but it's so hard not to believe myself. I wash my hands and I try to stare behind my eyes into the mirror, and I check all the other stalls, sure I'm not alone, but it's just me in there.

I navigate back to the table. "Are we about ready?"

We pay the bill and head out. The small mass of us shifts as we walk. When lawns border the sidewalk, James walks in the grass beside Connie and me. When the buildings and fences crowd in, he falls behind. When we pass someone, we form a single-file line and then reswarm.

On Connie's block, I say, "Have you noticed that return trips always take less time? Like didn't the walk home feel so much shorter than the walk to the restaurant?"

"It's all about perception," James says. "We were hungry. You and I weren't sure of where we were going. Now, we're full and drunk. We know the way."

"I know. I didn't think that it actually took less time," I say. "But it *feels* like it does. Are you guys up for watching a movie tonight?"

"Sure." Connie pushes open the door. "Whatever you want, chickadees."

She flips on the light and we see it right away. The wall of her front hallway is coated in a childlike scrawl. Circles and marks come together to make faces forming a column of eyes, nose, mouth, followed by another nose beneath and a set of eyes below that, then a nose, a mouth. A correctly oriented face followed by an inversion of that face, and again.

Connie's brow furrows. She turns to James and says the obvious. "What is this?"

"What do you mean? I didn't do that," James says.

My breathing becomes quick, and I find the sofa to sit down. "It has to be," I say. I feel as if I might throw up or pass out. I hear the ringing drone, but I'm not in the house so I tell myself it's in my head.

James sits down beside me, his head in his hands. "Fuck, fuck, fuck, fuck, *fuck*."

"It's like that drawing in your bedroom. Why are you doing it, James? You did this before we went to dinner? Why? You fucked up my wall," Connie says.

James stands and snaps at Connie, "I don't make those drawings in our house, Connie, and I didn't make this one either. Jesus Christ!" He slams back down on the cushion beside me, and my stomach jerks.

Connie says, "I really do hope that's true. I invited you here. I hope you're not fucking with me, because that would be sick, James. If it's not you, then I'm phoning the police. Last chance to own up." She waits a moment, but James says nothing. "Okay . . . *Shit*," she says as if she wishes it were James who did it. "Fuck, that means someone was in my *house*?" She lets out a frustrated cry and punches a number into her phone, heading for the kitchen.

"We're doomed," I say to James. "Whatever this thing is, it's inside of us now. We can't shake it."

James refuses to respond. He takes out his own phone and goes to the wall to take pictures. I watch him and wish he'd say *something*, but his anger has stuffed him so full, the words can't get out. Finally, the sobs pulse out of me, like an artery opened. I pull myself into a ball and hide my face in the corner of Connie's couch, squeezing a pillow with all my might.

Connie returns to the living room. "The police said they'll be over to take a look." She doesn't comfort me or wait for me to stop crying. "I'm sorry, guys. I can't stay here tonight. I'm going to call my cousin to see if I can go there."

"I'm so sorry," I wrench out through uneven breaths. "We're going." I stop myself. "Or we can stay until the police get here if you want."

"Stay." I look up at her. I don't understand how she's able to be so calm. Rather than fear or anger, I see the confusion in her face, a lack of understanding, and it's clear that Connie hadn't believed until now. Connie had listened to my stories, but she thought none of it could be as real as I said. "What the *fuck*," she keeps exhaling on repeat. She still thinks she might find an answer.

64

CONNIE FROWNS WHILE we wait for the police to arrive. Two patrolmen show up, but one is the cop with the furrow of scar down his cheek. He catches sight of me on the couch. "You're the neighbors of that missing guy."

"That's right," I say, weary.

"What are you doing here?"

Julie senses hostility. She stands, trying to protect me. "We were staying with Connie for the night."

"Is that right? Your husband really attracts trouble, huh?" He winks at Julie. "Maybe time for an upgrade."

I look for a wedding ring. I don't find one. "I think that's enough, Officer," I say, stepping forward.

He holds a hand up. "It's all in good fun." He turns back to his partner. They take photos. They write down the chain of events as Connie relays them. I wait for Connie to mention the drawings in our home. She keeps silent on this front, though.

"Always best to lock your house, Ms. Abbatacola," the officer reminds her.

"Lesson learned." Connie bites her upper lip. She holds the door open. The cops exit. When she shuts the door, she triple-checks the lock and the dead bolt.

We exchange apologies again.

"I want to get out of here. I'm sorry to kick you out." Our bags sit by the door. I don't know when Connie retrieved them.

"Please don't apologize," Julie says. "Clearly, we're to blame."

We drive the short distance home. I feel the dread crowd between us.

I go inside. Julie pulls out glasses. She runs the tap. "The not knowing is paralyzing."

She sits down at the table with me. She takes a sip. I see blossoms of algae floating in the water. A scummy layer coats the glass. Julie gags. She runs to the sink. She throws up what she's just swallowed. "What was that?" she gasps. "What did I drink?"

I stand back. I inspect Julie's glass. "It looked normal before you drank out of it."

Julie freezes. I can tell she's searching her brain for something. "Bad behavior heralds ruin," Julie whispers. I ask her to repeat herself. "Bad behavior heralds ruin. I've been reading up on hauntings. If a spirit knows you've been doing bad things, they'll have a harder time leaving you alone. They want your bad energy out of their space."

"Oh my God. You're reading a book about ghosts like it's fact?"

"We're going to make lists," Julie says. "Of all the bad we've done and all the bad this house has done back to us. We're going to track this thing. We're going to hunt it down, intrigue it, and rip it out of here."

Julie starts taping pieces of paper to the wall. She sticks a black stripe of gaff tape through the middle of the sheets. Two rows. "I'll write all the ways I've screwed up above the tape. You write yours below, and in the second row, we'll write all of the weird shit that's happened to us or that we've seen or heard or felt."

She hands me a permanent marker. She starts writing.

"I don't think I can keep straight what's happened to you or me. At this point, my experiences are yours."

"Write that down." Julie turns back to the wall. She scribbles furiously.

65

WE ARE SILENT, recording all of our sins and grievances, until I look back to see what James writes and I freeze. James is scrawling, like he thinks he's writing something, but all I see are wavy lines of nonsensical script.

"James!" He pauses and looks at me, tucks his top lip around his teeth, pulling his face longer. I haven't seen him do this before, and it makes his face strange, unfamiliar to me. "What are you doing?"

"Writing down what I've done and what I've seen, like you said."

I look at his marks and then at the way the lids have pulled back around his eyes, trying to get him to see what I see, and then I realize that maybe it's me. Maybe it's me that's seeing what he is doing as wrong, and I panic. "Those are words?"

James stands up straighter, caps his marker. "They are."

"Are my words also words?"

James looks at the wall and nods. "Yep."

"James, can you read your list to me?" I feel like I might pass out.

James looks pretty calm for what seems like another impossibility. "Let's see. Wrongdoings: 'I gambled away my money. Thought I slept in a cave but I woke up at home. Stendhal syndrome at art museum. Pulled house inside out.'" I watch him read. He presses a finger to the wall to follow along, but I can't reconcile the marks with the words he's speaking. "'I repaired everything again. I saw a double of Julie in the guest bedroom. I interpreted children's play as threatening. I spied on our neighbor, Rolf, and let myself into his home. I quit my job. I nearly drowned myself.' That's all I've got so far." He looks at me expectantly, nervously.

It takes me a moment to emerge from my terror at not being able to read his words. "You quit your job?" I register surprise and loss, not anger.

He looks away. "It wasn't the right place for me."

"When?"

"About two weeks ago."

"But you leave the house every day. Where do you go?"

"I go to the library to look for new jobs. I wanted to have another lined up by the time I told you. I knew you'd be mad."

"Yes! Yes, I am! First the gambling, and now this? Are we in this together or not? Do I know you?" My lips smile, a forced consolation. I refocus. "James, why are all of those things listed under *Sins*? You're not responsible for all of that."

"I don't want to believe that I'm not in control, Julie. I want to believe that I can resist it. I have the power to stop it or at

least not help it along. Maybe that's why I quit the job. I want to take charge again." His eyes well up and he looks away.

"But do you have control now? Or are you just taking your chances?"

He gulps and grabs hold of his reason. "If something bad is going to happen, I'd like to believe that I'm not a part of it. If I'm doing something wrong, I think I'm culpable for everything else that goes off the rails."

"James, we are not responsible for this."

"You just said we were. That our bad behavior was causing spirits to act out."

"Right, but not all of it is us," I say, bereft.

"I think it is, Jules. I think we're haunting ourselves. We're pulling ourselves apart. We're noticing gaps and stepping into them instead of avoiding them."

I shake my head violently, landing my face in my hands. "What what what what what what what what are you saying? What the hell are you saying? What the fuck, James? I thought we were on the same page. Because *I* can't control what's going on. Maybe *you* can, but I can't. Maybe this is all you then, James. Maybe you're the one I need to leave behind. Is that it?"

I am not accustomed to seeing hurt register on James's face. "Julie, it's both of us. We're doing it together. It's like a closed circuit. We're destroying ourselves."

"No." I tear the pages down and ball them up, and the ends of the black tape stick to my palms, but I free myself and whip the balls of paper at the wall. "No, that is not it."

66

JULIE AND I sleep in different corners of the house. We form an anagram of our regular nights. I curl myself on our bed. Julie sprawls her body across the sofa. In the middle of the night, I go down to the living room. I sit on the arm of the couch.

Julie rouses. "How long have you been there?"

"I'm sorry," I say. "I believe you and trust you, but so much of this situation is unbelievable. If I can't imagine I'm in control of at least myself, where do we end up?"

She sighs. She asks me to get her a drink of water.

"I think you should probably get it yourself. By the time I bring a glass to you it'll be full of mold."

She walks to the kitchen. She skips the glass entirely. She turns on the faucet and holds her lips to the stream of water. I flip the light on. Julie spits. I go to the sink. I see the greenish slime still sticking to the steel basin. The water coming out of the faucet looks clear. I wonder if a moldy clump loosened in the pipe. Is the water reacting to some catalyst in Julie's mouth? I ask if the mold might be growing inside us.

"Everything feels wrong," Julie says. "I can't even recognize a mistake anymore, you know? When everything feels so out of sorts, I can't recognize what it is that's tipping the balance. Everywhere I look, I'm trying to figure out how I'm being fooled. I'm suspicious of everything. It's exhausting."

"I know." She wraps her arms around my waist and presses her cheek to my chest, and I stroke her hair and lean my lips down to her hairline. "If we believe it's us, I know how to change myself, you know? If it's something else, I don't see a way out. Even if we leave, it's following us."

"I hear you." Julie squeezes tighter.

67

"AND THEN SOMETIMES I think, 'What if it's all a prank?'"
James says.

I release my grip. "What?"

"It's hard not to consider: What if you're messing with me?
Or it's like a *Scooby-Doo* episode where the angry villain who
lives next door is trying to force us out and he's rigged these
elaborate illusions?"

I feel near tears. "James, are you saying this has all been a
hoax?"

"I'm sorry, no," he says. "But I guess I wish it was. Imagine."

Something shifts in my mind, and James looks unusual,
like my husband is being played by another actor, like swapped-
out kids in a sitcom series. "You're in on it," I say, and he looks
at me with concern in his eyes. "Whatever is going on here, it's
talking you into believing it and spreading its doctrine."

"Julie, what are you talking about? That's not what I'm say-he's come, he is sensitive, and he doesn't need me seeking some arrival on top of him, and knowing that this is for me alone is enough to send my head back and I roll off and remember what happened earlier and who blames whom. I turn from him and snarl and he growls back.

The bed is hotter when he's in it, and I hate that, but it's a hate I'd rather not do without. In other words, I love hating his presence when it means a few degrees under a blanket. Even if I don't recognize him right now, I can recognize the heat coming off his body. Even though I don't recognize him, I am growing to recognize myself. I say, "Tell me how you'll hurt me and I'll tell you how I'll respond," but he has gone quiet.

I shut my eyes for a long time without sleep, and when I open them, I see the murky outline of someone, more the deep shade of a figure on the darkness than the lightness of a human form. "James." I feel for him beside me, but can't find him in the bed, so I allow my mind to confirm the figure must be him, but still I ask, "James, is that you?" The figure retreats and then I hear a rolling slide and a bump, like a pocket door closing itself and I can't see the dim cloud anymore and I remember when I was caught in the wall, and I stand and flip the light on, but the wall is as it was after I emerged: solid, unseamed. On the nightstand, though, the journal has been returned, but without the loose pages packed into the front. I open it to find the rolling text, illegible like James's handwriting on the wall, or could it be that James's handwriting is like what I'd seen in the book? I hear questions in my mind but have the strange sensation that they are not mine. Could I be tripping on a single burn scar? Skipping around the same groove? A record needle tracing an

ing. I'm saying, we're making it up without intending to, not that we're trying to manipulate one another."

"You just said you're the one making this happen. Why won't I listen? You have control over all of this. It makes sense now. Most times, I don't even feel like I'm talking to *you*. I feel like I'm speaking with something you've been convinced of. But I don't know where *you* are. I can't trust *you*." Only after I've said these words do I feel how true they sound, and my breath leaves, my sight disappears, returns.

He swings his head back and forth rapidly, as if he's trying to get rid of something, erase a thought. I can almost see his train change tracks, avoiding my accusations. "Well, why should I believe *you*? You've acted out as much as I have in the past few months." He counts on his fingers. "You keep passing out. You started dreaming of bodies covered in fingers. You *say* you haven't been doing the drawings, but why should I trust you? And then all of this business with Rolf missing. You probably know where he is!"

"It's all a joke!" I can't get the thought out of my mind. "Just kidding!" I laugh. I can feel the cruelty set my mouth in a grin. "How does it feel? Just kidding!"

"Yeah, it's all a ruse." James's eyes go dead as he condescends. "That's exactly what I was trying to say. So glad you understand me so *fully*." He turns as if he's going to leave the room, but comes back. "Thanks so much for your undying *support*, Julie. You've been so understanding. But, yes, the joke's on you! Everything I do, I'm just trying to mess with you." He steps back, throws his hands up, provoking some kind of response. "The jig is up! You're on *Candid Camera*! JK! April Fools'!

April Fools' your fucking cervix and April Fools' this house opening itself to us and April Fools' whatever it is that's growing here. April-fucking-Fools', Julie! Yep, that's what I meant."

I sob, terrified now of this man, convinced of his complicity. I'm backed into a corner of the counter while he rails inches from my face. I'm not even fighting back, just taking the verbal punches this moment throws at me, but my body fatigues. I push him away and turn to lean against the counter and quake.

"Just kidding," James chokes out, and I hear him walk away, hear the basement door open, his steps down the stairs.

"Just kidding!" I scream, and bang my sore fists on the granite countertop.

68

I GO TO bed alone and sleep quickly with vivid dreams of soured lilies and the sick, brown smell of turned hydrangeas, transformed from petals to litter.

I hear steps on the stairs and our bedroom door swings wide and then James slides one foot and then another into bed, but it's not James, it's both him and not him. It's the true him that's been hidden from me all this time, not the fake him that is familiar to me, and I waste no time in rolling onto him and pushing my face into his. I let his tongue meet mine and I let his mouth find my neck and suck and bite and I drag his hand to where I'm wet. I grasp at the hairs on his head and make promises with the way I press him and I reach a hand down and shove him inside me and I should know it's too much, but I don't care. I grind into him recklessly and hear the breaths that I know mean he's had his fill, but I continue, and his fingers work more quickly to help me make the same decision, because once

error? I'm making my way through the same paths of the maze repeatedly. I feel my mind rush in and then disperse. I climb into bed and pull myself back together, like metal filings to a magnet, and by the time I fall asleep, light already sneaks through the windows.

When I wake, I'm sure I'll be late for work, so I lug myself to the bathroom and splash water on my face and blink the water from my eyes and I see it: the glowing purple of a bruise on my neck. I touch the mirror and remember the night before and remember James's mouth there and my shoulders sink with relief because a hickey is nothing to worry about. It can't tell me stories I don't want to hear, and I return to the bedroom and hunt for a scarf that I can pass off as a choice even in the warm weather.

I feel the sun through the windows, the room already starting to stink with the sneaking spores. I slide a dress down my body and pause, looking at James's side of the bed, and sit down and run my hand over the sheets and try to imagine the warmth of him still there, a clue about when he left, but no matter how assuredly my hand tries to divine the heat, it turns up nothing, and I worry for only a moment more and head out.

At work, Connie recognizes the scarf for what it is immediately. "Show me."

"It's not what you think." I realize how I sound and lower my voice. "This one's a hickey."

"Seriously?" She tries to connect the dots of how the night could end that way.

I bow my head, and when I move, I feel a heavy ache rooting itself in my spine. "We fought. He was saying things that made me think I didn't even know him, blaming himself, and I just can't accept that. He stalked down to the basement and I fell asleep, but I woke up when he came to bed and he still seemed like some other person, but I felt this"—I pause and just say it—"this desire, this impulse to seize the chance to sleep with someone new, even though it was still James, and I acted. Hence . . ." I fan my fingers beside my neck.

"Jesus. If he's so set on taking the blame, maybe he is to blame? He was the last one in my house before that drawing showed up. I don't want to call your husband a liar, but something is going on with him. And *that* is one hell of a hickey, Jules." She moves in closer to inspect.

My hand involuntarily travels to it, and even that gentle, absentminded touch sends the dull throb spiking higher, but despite this surprising hurt, I say, "It's a regular old hickey. No big deal. It's embarrassing, but my dignity has survived worse. How was the rest of your night? I feel like no matter what James's deal is, we're to blame somehow. When will you be able to stay at home again?"

Connie keeps her eyes on the hickey. "It's fine. My cousin's going to help me paint over the vandalism tonight and then she's going to stay with me for a night or two until I feel better."

"I'm so sorry," I say. I can't help myself.

"Julie." Connie squints and turns me to the side. "I don't think this is just a hickey. It stretches from behind your ear and all the way down to below your clavicle." She points to a spot under the collar of my shirtdress and I angle my head to try to see and there it is. The bruise is pushing at its boundaries, expanding as I watch. I think of the way James grabbed my shoulder on our walk to the restaurant and pull my collar wider to see the bruise on my neck advancing toward the one on my shoulder. They rush for each other at a glacial pace. I feel my eyes well up with fury that I've done this to myself. I let the hickey happen and now the bruise can grow from there. Is it harder to begin something or to keep it going? My mind races with examples that make both statements feel true and I think of how it's easy to keep dating a person but hard to keep the relationship alive once you've hit a tough spot. Had I provided a host or would it have found me anyway?

Connie swipes back the hair behind my ear and leans in. "It continues past your hairline, Julie. Jesus."

I bite my lip to keep from crying. "Get to work. I'll deal with this later. No use worrying about it now. It's not like it's anything new."

Connie walks away, like I've let her down.

I see an email from my boss, and my stomach drops. I'm worried he'll have read the plan for the product I drew up while I was at home and see all the weaknesses, all the details I should have had time to figure out while I was out of the office, the specifications I took educated guesses on rather than researching. "Looks like a great start. Let's meet as a team later this week to discuss" is all the email says, and I wonder if I'm working too hard most of the time, if it's always me inviting trouble.

69

IN MY DARKROOM, I dream of returning to the city. The cool basement air reminds me of the air-conditioned bar. The noon sun muted by the dark plastic sunshade pulled down over the windows. The chilled feeling of the lacquered oak beneath my forearms. The prickle of freshly poured lager down my throat as I examine the names of the horses on the betting sheet. The rush at either win or loss, the extremity of feeling assured, controlled in all but outcome. I long for the comfort of placing my worry on a race rather than this real life crumbling around me.

The doorbell rings and I make my way upstairs. Through the glass I can see the detectives' car out front. I wonder if they've found Rolf.

I swing the door open. "What can I do for you, Detectives?"

"Can we come in?" asks O'Neill.

"Please." I step aside. I open the door wide. They hover for a moment before I lead them to the dining room.

They eye me. "Did we wake you?"

"No, no. I was working in the basement. What is this about?"

Poremski's eyes move to the crumpled sheets of paper on the floor, covered in our grievances. O'Neill asks, "What's all this?"

I curse myself for bringing them into this room. I stumble over myself. "My wife and I . . . we had a fight. She wanted to do some kind of . . . writing exercise together to try to work things out." I laugh, performing the dismissiveness I think is expected of me. "Anything she says so we can move on already, right?"

They nod tentatively. O'Neill says, "And that would have been before or after you visited Connie Abbatacola's house?"

"After." Of course this is about Connie. I had nearly forgotten. Obviously Officer Scarface passed the word on that we were at Connie's.

"Do you mind if we take a look around?" O'Neill asks.

I feel fear at what they might find, what we've failed to hide. I don't see a way around it. "Is something the matter, Officer? Have Julie and I done something wrong?"

"No, no. Where *is* your wife?"

"At work?" I phrase it like a question. I can't be sure. It seems like the most likely answer.

I follow the pair of them upstairs. They peek into the guest room briefly before moving on. In our bedroom, they pause. They note the figure drawn on the wall. They can't help but exchange a glance. Poremski steps out of the room to make a call. O'Neill looks at me. He gestures toward the wall. "What can you tell me about that?"

I panic inside. I know what his mind is telling him. This figure looks like the one in Connie's entryway. They must be related. It only makes sense that it's me who's drawn both. I wonder if Connie told them about this drawing. Could she have asked them to come take a look? "These keep showing up in our house, too. I assumed it was my wife making them. She thought it was me. Neither of us is correct, from what I understand."

"And you haven't reported them?" O'Neill appears to be giving me the benefit of the doubt. He wants to hear a good reason why we would keep this information to ourselves.

"Like I said, we both thought the other was playing a trick. We've been going through a lot." I pause and then decide to move in a direction that might discount my reliability, but also take some heat off us. "Honestly, we think this house is haunted. Everyone in town keeps saying as much. We keep looking for another reasonable explanation, though. We don't really believe in that sort of stuff. We've been trying to work through it on our own. We're not getting very far. We need help."

O'Neill's eyes bug out for a moment in frustration. He does not want to hear about our marital problems. He is a logical man. I am talking in riddles. "Mr. Khoury, I'm going to need you to be more explicit. What is it you need help with? Are you in danger? Are you unwell? Is there something more we should know?"

I realize then that the detective thinks we might not have reported the drawings because we have something else that we're trying to hide. He believes we have evidence of some crime we have or haven't committed. In that same moment I realize there's no way to say, believably, without attracting more suspicion, *We haven't done anything.* Instead, I say, "My wife and I, I believe we've both taken this move rather hard. I don't know if it's depression, paranoia, anxiety. We're not ourselves. It's been complicated by some strange stuff happening in the house. Sounds we hear. We think we see things. There are all of these hidden storage areas we keep finding. We haven't settled in like we hoped."

Poremski returns to the room to take pictures of the drawings. O'Neill watches him for a moment. Then he looks at me. "Mr. Khoury, I think you and your wife need to get ahold of yourselves. If you think you need help doing that, I suggest you talk to a *doctor* or a *social worker* who can help you work through your issues. In the meantime, we're going downstairs, and you're going to tell me everything you can remember about when this drawing showed up and the circumstances around it."

I think about whether I should mention that we saw drawings like these in the cave, too. I tell myself that the writing on the walls of the cave is gone now, so sharing this would only make us seem more deluded.

I have the urge to apologize. I have the itch to say, *This isn't enough. I think you're the one who can help.* Instead, I allow the detectives to lead the way out of the room.

70

AT WORK I search a million terms trying to find an answer: bruises; primitive drawings; graphomania; contusions; filth; mold; blooms; infestation; magic tricks; haunting; shallow grave; spying; elder neighbor care; death; resurrection; caves. I search our names and our address but am accustomed to those results.

Nothing compelling turns up. I go to our team meeting to discuss the new product and explain my findings. People volunteer to look into different pieces of the puzzle, and I'm grateful I don't need to run down the list of assignments I'd drawn up. A good team member can see a bigger picture and figure out his or her place. My coworker in publicity suggests different approaches for marketing the product and my mind wanders back to the search I'd been doing before the meeting. I turn to my laptop screen and enter all of the terms I'd thought of into the search bar at once and what returns shuts up my curiosity. I click into the image search, and the results become even more real. There, in picture after picture, are James and then me and then the house and then Rolf and then the cave and then the walls of the cave flush with scribbles and the documentation shots of my bruises and then the drawings on the walls of the house and then a picture of me last night in bed with a man I don't recognize but know must be my husband and then and then and then.

My hearing blacks out, and I close my computer. "I'm sorry, if you'll excuse me, I have a call I need to run to." I hope no one will notice that it's nowhere near the end of the hour. I pray no one will think it's strange that I scheduled a call to overlap with an internal meeting I set up. If they ask, I will say I'm so busy, I'm running into myself.

71

THE POLICE CAR pulls away. I exit through the back door. I can't stand to be in the house for another minute. I'm pushed out. The trees are fewer than before. The ones that have lasted are thick and tall like redwoods. I stare up through the undergrowth. The children have returned. They are rumbling now at each other. They sit at the ends of branches that don't look as if they can hold their weight. They hold hands with the children in the trees beside them. I think of the game KerPlunk, where thin plastic sticks are inserted in a clear tube. Marbles balance on top of the intersections. The goal is to pull out the sticks without letting the marbles drop. Eventually all the orbs will fall, though. There is no way to balance slick glass on pure air.

I imagine the branches giving way. The children scattershot through the forest.

I call up to them. I ask if they need help. Their eyes shift down toward me. Their growls continue.

I go back to the edge of the yard. I look for what Julie thought was a grave. I consider burying myself there. The idea of it sounds secure to me. It would be satisfying to be locked in. I can sense the comfort of being weighed down. I think of a killer putting a victim in a bathtub and filling the bathtub with concrete. I pause on my way to the back door to try to imagine the pain that would arise from not being able to move. I try and try. It's not there in the memories of my body.

I return to the house and realize I've left the back door wide-open. We're so certain of our fear that we don't think in those binaries anymore: inside outside, good evil, known unknown, fact fiction. There's nothing to eliminate. There's no way for us to know the same thing with our separate brains.

I fill a glass with water. I inspect it for spots of mold. I stare out of this container we've placed ourselves in. From every window I can see the neighbor's house, the woods out back and to the side, the street, all at once, from every view. I imagine our home folded out like a map of the earth. I look out instead of in. I wonder where the break falls, like that scar that pulls the Pacific Ocean in half so we can see the whole flat world in a single glance. I think of the hidden rooms. I try to piece together a blueprint in my head. When the spaces don't fit together, my mind breaks them apart, like resetting a bone.

I notice a shadow move in the house next door. Sure enough, there is Rolf's face in the window. He stares at me for a moment, then is gone. I am wishing that I had proof. Whom would I show it to? I am reevaluating my allegiances.

72

I KNOW ON Rolf's door. I wonder if I actually saw him. I consider calling the police. I don't know if what I have to tell them is truth, though.

What I do instead is return to the basement of my own home. I start pawing at the walls. I shove the cabinet out of the way to look at the stain. I grab a sledgehammer from the workbench. I barrel through the plaster. Nothing is hiding behind it as I'd hoped. The stalactite and stalagmite growths of dripping minerals from the edge of the foundation gather where the beads drop and land. I'm reminded of the subway stations back in the city. The growth is so gradual. The natural fights its way into our man-made world.

I run my hands around the rest of the basement walls. I see a shadow beneath the paint at the bottom of the stairs. I scratch at the wall with my fingers. The plaster lodges under my nails, stinging. I traipse to the workbench again. I rifle through the mess of my previous disturbances. I find sandpaper.

I will perform a dig. I will rough away the top layer of paint. I will uncover a truth.

I start wiping at the wall with the coarse square. The faint gray line becomes darker. I follow the line. I scratch down its length, like driving slowly in a snowstorm.

What I uncover is another face. It is not unlike the others that have shown up more plainly, a squared-off circle of sorts. I swipe at the middle. I find its crude features. I wonder if what I'm doing counts as drawing. Like the wood being carved away from a printing block, am I bringing these figures into being after all? Have I done this before?

I continue scratching. I find more of them: faces, a few stretching themselves down to shoulders. The plaster is thin in spots. A hole forms itself perfectly in the center of an eye or in the maw of a mouth. I try to look beyond them to see what is on the other side of this wall. My logical mind tells me it should be the furnace room.

I can't see anything but darkness. I tell myself to get a flashlight. I obey.

I return downstairs. Piles of plaster dust the ground. I should have put on a mask. I think of what was trapped behind the walls that I might have released. I think of the mold crawling down my throat.

I pull myself into a formation. One arm aims the flashlight through a hole above my head. My eye is situated at another opening. I flip the switch in my hand.

The space I find is not the furnace room. It's a skinny path between walls. Maybe even a slim hallway. It's big enough that a person could walk through it by shuffling sideways.

A bed, narrow as an army cot. Pillows and dolls, covered in

filth, litter the floor. Unframed photographs leaf the walls. My eyesight goes in and out. I see a class picture of Julie's. I find a photo of my family on the beach when I was a teenager. A snapshot of a young girl I don't know, blinking against the sun. I feel certain that the picture of a man fishing on a familiar-looking dock is Rolf.

73

I'M HIDING OUT in the floor's shared ladies' room when Connie finds me. She recognizes my shoes under the door and knocks. I panic and try not to answer. My head is unspun. I feel parched from crying. Too disoriented to understand why the walls are thumping at me, and too paralyzed to slide back the lock. She makes the sacrifice of allowing her knees to touch the tile so that she can peer under the stall's door to find me sitting on the closed toilet seat, my face streaked with tears. "Can you unlock the door, Julie?" When I don't move, she slithers under, saying, "I must really care." She struggles to stand, unlocks the door, but doesn't try to maneuver out yet. "You can't hide in here all day, Julie. What happened? You were holding it together."

"More. More since you found the new bruise."

"What more?"

I'm feeling protective of myself again and look down instead of answering.

"It's okay. You've got to pull it together, though. People are looking for you." She leads me out of the stall and makes me splash water on my face. She hands me a paper towel to dry it.

In the mirror, I catch sight of my face, looking as if my plates have shifted, as if half my face were on a different level from the rest.

"Ready?"

I follow Connie out of the bathroom.

While we're walking the concrete hall back to the office, I see the two detectives flash a badge at the front door and the office manager points at me, though I would bet Connie wonders if she's pointing at her, too, and they stride toward us. "Ms. Abbatacola, I hope you're well this morning. Mrs. Khoury, it's you we're hoping to talk to. Is there somewhere we could speak privately?"

I lead them to the big conference room next to the entrance.

"We're sorry to disturb your workday, Mrs. Khoury. We have a few questions. First, do you recognize these photos?"

The taller detective, O'Neill, shows me pictures of the drawings on the wall of our bedroom and I wonder what else they know. All of it? The way the search engine has bounced my entire life back to me as if I were being surveilled? I convince myself it's nothing so complicated. They must have stopped at the house and James was home to let them in. I pause and know there is only one way to answer their question. "I do."

"And can you tell us who made these drawings?" The detective cocks his head to the side.

"I thought it was my husband, but he denies it."

"And you saw the drawings that showed up on the wall of Ms. Abbatacola's house, right?"

I see where he's headed and believe I'll gain credibility if

I get there first. "I did, and, yes, they look like the ones in our bedroom."

"But you didn't inform us of the drawings that appeared on the wall of your bedroom?"

I wonder if the shorter one, Poremski, ever talks. He doesn't look like the muscle between them, and I look him up and down trying to figure out what part he plays, before turning back to the one asking the questions. "Like I said, I thought that my husband was playing a trick on me, so no."

"But not even after you saw the vandalism in the home of your friend?"

There's a knock at the door and my coworker, Tim, peeks his head in. "Whoa, I'm sorry! I'll book another room!" He ducks out.

"I'm not sure I have a good answer for you." All of my other worries show up again, and I change tacks: "Have you found our neighbor yet?"

"We haven't. I'll take that to mean you also haven't seen him?"

I rub my forehead. "No."

"Okay, Mrs. Khoury. That's all for now. Please let us know if you think of anything else that might be helpful."

"Did you talk to my husband?" I have the urge to know that our stories match up.

"We did."

"And?"

"I'm sure he'll fill you in," one of the detectives says, and they excuse themselves.

74

I WANT TO assume Julie is the one to blame because it feels easy and possible. All of the signs indicate I'm the one doing the drawings. Even alone in the basement, looking at myself, I come in and out of focus as the culprit. I wonder if I'm losing my grip. I refuse to believe it. I let myself accuse Julie instead. I don't hold back. I flood with all the pent-up anger that she moved us to this tiny town. I blame her for stopping me from gambling. I blame her for thinking it was a problem. If I'd had a little more time, my luck would have turned around. I think of the bruises on her body. There's no reason for them. I imagine her running herself into walls. She makes the marks appear. She was never trapped in a secret room as she says. Maybe there is a grave in the backyard. Maybe it's filled with the body of Rolf. I'm furious that, through all of this, she's dismissed my fears and demanded sympathy and comfort for her own. I have visions of the police arriving and taking me away for our neighbor's murder. I imagine Julie looking at me as if I've disappointed her. That feeling is so familiar I do the only thing I can think of to avoid it.

That afternoon I pretend to be Julie. I write letters confessing to causing all of this. I explain how she did it. I write that she drugged me. She clawed holes in the walls. She hid Rolf's body. She made every drawing. Every sentence paints a motive. She did it for proof of life. She did it to scare me off. She did it as revenge for my misdeeds. She wanted to test her limits. She wanted to teach me. She wanted to teach herself.

I try to mimic her handwriting. I get pretty close. I throw away the ones that look least accurate. I leave the good drafts on the table. I go back to the basement.

The holes I made in the wall are gone.

I can't see where they were. I don't know where to search. I run my hands along the surface. I don't find what I'm looking for. No wet plaster. I go to the tool bench in back. The drill is in place, the battery cool. The mop is dry. I sit down on the stairs in front of the wall. I try to convince myself that what I saw was real. My memory feels fuzzed out, coated. I think about grabbing the sledgehammer and confirming what I found behind the wall here. I rush through ways that Julie could be responsible for this. I look in the darkroom to see if she's hiding there. I call her name. And again. My mind keeps snapping into focus, knowing Julie isn't the one who fixed this wall. My thoughts blur again, but then I can see she's not guilty of the rest either. At least not all of it. I consider writing letters where I take the blame myself. Fatigue clarifies in me. I check the time to find it's only 6:00 p.m. Still, I call it a night.

I glance at the letters on the dining room table as I head upstairs. I should shred them. I should turn them into pulp before Julie gets home. Their edges are beginning to whorl. The air of the house spoils even crisp paper. I pause. I watch as one piece rolls itself into a tube. It rocks back and forth, ever so slightly, as if under an invisible hand. A sickening flicker. I reach the bedroom. I collapse on the foot of the bed. I contort.

75

JAMES OR NOT-JAMES doesn't respond when I call out, "Hello? . . . No? Nothing? You've wandered off again? Transformed into someone else I don't know? Left me here talking to myself?" I envision him pummeled by the tide at the lakefront, facedown in an alley somewhere. I think of him crawling back into the earth like a worm after rainfall.

The stench in the house has gone from awful to unbearable. On the table, I see sheets of loose-leaf curling themselves in the moist air, and on them I find my own handwriting laying bare confessions, saying I am to blame for all of the bullshit that's been going on in this house, sneaking crushed pills into the food and unscrewing pipes in the basement and clotting them with huge handfuls of mold and pinching my skin so hard it shows the deep colors of bursting blood vessels.

I do not remember writing these and the fright nerves through me as I wonder how and why they exist. I take them out onto the deck with me because I think I might choke on the air of the house and I sit on the step and read through them again and wonder at what I don't know or can't remember about myself. Certainly James or not-James read them and that is why he has gone and while I'm reading about the bruises, my hands go to their evidence and I'm shocked at how paranoid and frantic I sound in the letters, each one a bit different, giving alternative reasons for why I've done what I've done, as if what the pages contain isn't truth, but an attempt to find answers by claiming guilt.

I ask myself what I should do, because if I leave the letters out, it's like saying I agree with them, that I accept that these missives have been written in my hand. If I hide them, maybe nothing will come of it, but if someone finds them, if the detectives decide to gut the house looking for evidence, they'll be certain the confessions are true, hidden away for a moment of courage. I could burn them, but if I need them as evidence later, to show how I was being manipulated or how I was out of my mind or how their multiplicity proved that none of them was true, what would I do? I go into the house and bury them in James's office, in a file he won't look at again, a tax-return folder from years ago.

Let's pretend it's James who knows this secret instead of me and let's take away the blame. Is he trying to protect himself or me? Whom would I rather shelter than harm?

I walk upstairs and James's or not-James's body hulks at the foot of the bed like a pet. I strip and climb into bed, leaving the man who thinks he knows so much below me.

I look at us from the outside and think of the Google search as proof. My thoughts guide themselves like imitations. *If there was another voice in my head, what would it sound like?* I try out different inflections, like writing a script, until one of the voices comes through easy and clear, less like I'm making it up and more like I'm listening. I wonder if that's how those letters got written. I ask myself if the voice that wrote those letters is my own, my other voice, a not-Julie's, like James is not-James, if it was this other voice that took over for a while, thinking of the neighbor constantly, feeling what it is to be absent of one-self and worrying that my shape might shift the way the house seems to grow and shrink, the way the figures on the wall breathe, the way the bruises pulse with unusual life, the way the stains glow and dim and the pipes blossom, and I decide to keep a close eye on myself. I decide it is best if I note where I end and the world begins, boundaries to be defended.

I can feel the boggy gas traveling from James's or not-James's warm mouth toward me and it nails me down against my pillow. Are we always barely missing each other? Our edges brush. Our hairs stand on end, reaching.

"James," I say, and not-James emerges, looking smaller, like catching a hummingbird still. My eyelids feel thin, as if too much light is getting in. I pull his hand so his face tilts up at me on the mattress and I well over and feel the fluke of a second self filling me up.

"We can get through this, Julie. We don't have to give up."

My mind runs like hell from such empty reassurance and I croon to him, singing in my sweetest voice, forming notes and phrases with the threads in my throat: "If you can't breathe, punch a hole in the window. If you dive deep into the ocean and the pressure gets too great, beware your eardrums burst first and ring like so many coins from a slot machine and you wish your fortune away and you wonder what you thought you were missing, and your hearing starts to take the form of roots, spiraling deeper into your brain, looking for water. Minutes are measured with the beat of your blood, and someone holds your head against the mat a second too long, and the cartilage separates and your flesh fills with blood and hardens, like a sausage, fat and dense, and like that, the seedy vortex has shifted, and your head is coated in prayer, and half of your brain is filled with your slow, stuttering pulse, while the other side tries to sprint. Maybe morning is no special gift. Hostile darkness no longer taxing, just the norm. How dusk feels different than dawn despite the light measuring the same. Like the sun might be burning itself out. Like watching the day in—"

76

"—REVERSE. REACHING MORNING. The sun sinking in-stead. The puddles of dew retreating back into the lawn. The idea that you can feel anything correctly. A notion of perfect worth-lessness. Something negative being flawless. A mold depressing itself to take in the media, space that must be emptied before it can be filled. The mold breaking around the sculpture but the sculpture holding still. The cage door opens and the bird stays put. The walls pull apart and the floors stack in place like pan-cakes. Shadows forming chalkier in the dusty evening than in the plump, damp morning. How hard it is to have surprising feelings when you know someone is watching. Being startled out of sleep by the sensation of falling. No forcing yourself to feel. How out of havoc and anger and threats can come venera-tion. How we think of God as old and all of our saviors seem to die young, turning over inside themselves while the world has them pinned."

I listen to Julie run herself out. I recognize this jag of her mind as something close to what my own did when I was stalled in front of that photograph at the museum and when I let myself lie down in the water. As a driver in a figurative ten-car pile-up, I can tell if I am going to live. Watching it happen beside me now, I am searching a spiderwebbed windshield for my wife. I can't know if she will be okay. That broken monologue whirs out into the space between us. The singing has turned into a chanting, like the drone of the house pulled into focus. I drag her in close to me to shrink the gap. "Julie, stop. Shh." She jerks away. Her face is her own, but behind her eyes is something unfamiliar. Her pupils have ballooned. The whites of her eyes glow.

"How we rehearse and consider what to keep private and what to share. How this transforms. How being completely open with your opinions and feelings can strip away intimacy, honesty traded for privacy. Switch to refusing to answer. How it can be hard to imagine yourself a hero with all of your faults laid plain. Keeping secrets so you have something to share. How a priest might lose control of the secrets he's been given. How a priest might hold so many stories while also creating his own. How a therapist might whisper the things she knows into her pillow at night to make room for more. Compassion fatigue. How there is no limit to how many times you can tell a person, *I understand*. How it might still not be enough. How language lies mostly in the flourishes that catch our ears. How language can sometimes only be heard in its consequences. How it can't stop being heard after that. How it might be easier to know what to say than when not to speak. How both silence and speech can expand until you're tightly in a corner. How contagious intensity deserves a name of its own. How only one of you might not need the other. How the other still needs to be needed. How impossible that situation becomes. How forgetting can pick up as much as it leaves behind. How necessary it is to reveal your disappointment. How life depends on it. How endings can't happen without this. How you're required to gaze at theft as it happens. How you mustn't look away. The wisdom of watching the candle flames lick the legs of the ladder and keeping quiet. How the strain becomes less frustrating and is no longer called to mind. How desire can be weakest when the fulfillment is most plausible."

The blankness of her eyes has filled her entire face. The Julie I know is nowhere to be found. A fire is lit inside her. I try to take her hand again. She rips it back. She shoves my shoulder. I stand and step away from her. Her strength startles me.

The chant has risen in pitch, still monotone, but earsplitting now. She screeches, the pace picking up at the end of her sentences, like an accelerating bouncing ball, until she's razed all the air from her lungs and fills the vacuum again. "The Lord has grabbed you and he has you in his sights and you must understand that he will not let you go and you must understand that you are belonged now and you must understand that you are not owned by yourself and that you have been filled up with a growth of spirit that is spread through words and images and I will provide you your new rule."

I keep hoping she might snap out of it. I keep hoping I might flip her switch. I speak more quietly. I aim to draw her out. "Julie. Please stop. You're really scaring me."

She tells me I don't know what scary is. If this is scary, I should see what the devil has in store. I should see what evil lurks in the unknown. She proclaims herself full of truth. She will not talk to an impostor. "Produce James," she howls. "I can see through your paltry imitation."

"It's me. *I am James.*" I move toward her again. She flinches. She tells me that I can touch her when the Lord shows up in my eyes. I pretend. I tell her I can feel him in my sight. I tell her that every bit of my being is filling with a new vision.

She calls me a liar. She says that when I feel it truly, she will know. We will spread this newfound honesty together. We will create our own language, like twins. Until then, she will beat me. Until the god in me comes out. Until she can trust that I will not corrupt her. She tells me to jump off the roof. If I am full of the dove of the holy spirit, then I will know how to fly my body to the ground.

I can't keep up the charade. "I am not ready for flight," I admit. I try to match her tone. I hope this might bring her closer to me. She brims with satisfaction. "But you, too, cannot fly," I say, eager to break her logic. She flees for the attic. Regret forms immediately, tight like a belt around my chest.

77

I SHOULD RACE after her. Instead I go to the backyard. I go to the dead lawn. Its blades loosen their fingers from the earth. The days of neglect compound beneath my feet. We have not watered the lawn. Or the tainted water of that wave Julie says besieged the house has suffocated the grass. I go outside to wait for a flight I don't believe will happen. Such radical instinct cannot be born so immediately.

Above me, she struggles to open the window. The layers of paint on paint stick until she squeezes through. I see the thick rope around her waist: a contingency plan, a strategy filled with harmful error. In this action I register a glimmer of hope. Her overzealous faith is an act. "Julie!"

She bares her teeth like a sick animal. "Your appreciation is a lie! I keep guns in my brain! I barge through reason to get to truth! I flush the cough syrup down the drain to be sure your voice runs out quicker. You are a minor flaw! I will descend on you and you will be erased!" She loses her footing for a moment on the sill. Even if she doesn't intend to jump, she might fall. I wake up. I grasp that only I can stop her. I run into the house cursing. I hear the bawl of her shouting. I don't hear the words. I climb the stairs in threes, racing. I reach the second floor. I see the parachute of her nightgown tumble past the hall window. I reverse. I sprint down the stairs to the yard. I have never moved so slowly.

I reemerge. It's like I'm staring through smudged glass. The rope hangs her a couple of feet above the ground. Her rag-doll fingertips and knees and toes dust the tips of the grass.

"Julie."

She groans.

I fear her spine has snapped. I think about not moving her. I move to call paramedics. I will let them make the decisions. On the stairs, though, I invert my instincts. I dart for the gardening shears. I am willing to take the blame if this is the wrong thing to do. It must be better to get her solidly on the ground instead of suspended like livestock being bled. It takes me several well-muscled attempts to cut through the rope. I catch her as she crumples. "Can you move?" She twists a little, whimpering. I see the farthest parts of her crimp and uncoil. Faith and confidence hide behind my fret.

Her hand travels to her abdomen. I peel the cloth up carefully. Already, the dark purple is forming in a thick band around her belly. The rope calls out of her more of what is lurking inside. The bruise ripples with proof.

78

I UNDERSTAND WHAT I'm doing and I have good reasons and it's not difficult to salvage beauty from the debacle, but I can't breathe so I can't explain this to James.

Each of my organs cinched, my pulse running ragged within me, I feel hammered out. That leap and fall flashing at the speed of hocus-pocus, *Hoc est corpus meum*, a prayer. My lungs well up like a soggy ashtray and my bladder sparks a fistful of anatomical tinsel. My bowels blistered, my womb bombed out.

Not-James holds me, staring in my eyes, willing me to swan out of the depth of myself again, but he leaves me and returns with a wheelbarrow and a mouth so pursed I swear it must be toothless and I am no longer my own.

"You will be safer in this." He lifts me, me without the will to balk, and he settles me into the cart, but my edges are too delicate for the broad metal and I try to trap the pain and arrest the scratch against my skin and focus instead on the blood

snuffing through my eardrums. I can tell how concerned not-
James is, but I wonder what it will take to get him to call an
ambulance, and I wish the blood would show through, because
all this bruising, the skin stretched to breaking, hides the truth.
I moan and not-James tells me this is a good sign, that at least
I'm alive, but I feel choked, and I want the flushing release of
my throat's opening to let in everything I need. I feel the route
of my injuries banging through my cranium and the deficien-
cies hiding deep in the center of my spine when not-James hoists
me over his shoulder at the front steps. "Almost inside," he says
at the top, but the pressure on my belly forces the sick out of my
mouth and it runs down not-James's back. He gets me in the
door and sets me on the couch and sees a deep red rim around
my mouth, the blood having found a way out, and he goes for
the phone and I feel pale time pass so deliberately as he demands
urgency from the operator. I want to be clean and I want to
beat off anyone who might help, but while I'm distracting my
mind with these desires, I lose myself and fall away and grunt as
if I were shot. I'm gone.

79

LIFE, EVEN AT its most dangerous, pushes through mundane details. Its procedural pace infuriates me. I am eager for development and answers. I am shocked by the profound dullness. Julie lies in a hospital bed. I immediately answer questions the doctors pose. Every request *I* make, however, takes hours to fulfill. In the ICU, the nurses and social workers and aides and doctors hear every bell and beep and respond with a measured hurry. I learn quickly to tune them out. I grow to assume nothing new is wrong.

I find it difficult to stay engaged. This alarms me. Surely, in these moments, I am concerned with nothing else aside from Julie's well-being. I operate at the height of myself. Yet, I find myself distracted. I get lost in what will come next and what I could have done differently. The doctors emerge with updates. I ask them to repeat themselves. It is hard to understand the simplest things. I can't stay trained on the present moment. I tune in and out like listening to a sermon. I keep saying things that make little sense. I notice my eyes scuffling around pages, unable to read them. I commit my signature to the line anyway. My breath lurches. I haul Julie's chances of surviving through my mind. I squat in my own belly. My viscera form teethfuls of nervous heat. I stare at a lightbulb until I'm blind. Sight knuckles the edges of the burning cataract.

Family visit in waves. Julie's parents show up. The adaptation of their daughter they find in her hospital bed disturbs them. My parents blow through. They make recommendations. They insist they'll return to see the house soon. Connie comes to the hospital. She has instructed Julie's other coworkers to leave us our privacy. My hope is that Julie can recover quickly. I hope people won't see this alternative version of her. I hope they won't hold it up as a comparison every day moving forward.

I avoid accepting Julie's condition. I disappear. I ask myself, *What is better? To accept the horror presented before you or search for a way out? To hunt in yourself for a comparable defect or to pull yourself tall and strong to support the correction of someone else's faults?*

There is no acceptable, untainted name for a wilderness of the mind. People will always wonder what to believe. They expect the stray inaccuracies to be looted out and abandoned. They expect the mind's voice to unstitch only when alone. When the seams rip, they look away.

80

IN THE HOSPITAL, I see not-James rattle and rummage for thousands of dollars to pay for the decision to help me live, the cost of health care an abstract inconvenience until it becomes real and necessary and he realizes how expensive the machines are that scour my system for threats, that empty every bit of me out, making a wire frame of my body, ignoring the years it took to make all of those cells. They flush in other people's versions of my blood and pull out my spoiled organs and replace them with flesh convinced from other persons. They find the filthy irregulars and kill them with chemicals and upriver energies, with no one coaxing the small of my back or giving me tempting eyes. They unscrew my beefy truths and find fires to put out and leave me in disarray. They mutter aloud and shine warm lights on parts of me that have never before seen their way out of the dark and blow warm air to stir my withered innards to dilation.

I wade through an unknown number of days—silent only in voice—in that hospital before I'm able to talk back, and by then, I know the doctors' questions, how they grease my palms with promises of survival and early release.

Where have I been living and working? My lungs are inflamed, full of a moldy growth.

What have I been doing and eating? A welter of iron paces my blood, but holes are opening in my veins allowing the deep red to seep and slam toward the surface, forming those bruises.

At first they think my mouth is full of meat scraps, but find it's my tongue and cheeks where my teeth wobbled through in the fall.

I'm unsure if I'm here because of my injuries or because of the impulse I had to throw myself off the roof, but either way, the doctors and nurses tell me stories of survivors with faith and determination as bright and shiny as new chrome, and they thunder their version of the kingdom of heaven into me, with absolute confidence, and I panic occasionally when I'm alone, and then I remember that someone is never far and fluster at that as well. When I'm made to walk through the halls, I think of carrying a ball of yarn to trace my way back. They wheel cots by the door like ponies storming. Bells constantly chime, enough to make my sleep shabby and my ability to wake nimble. I wonder at all the fingerprints in this place, the sly traces of blood no one will admit to, the dust waiting to edge into a wound despite custodial diligence.

When not-James is here, he spares no sigh, lets them all breathe into the room, his shoulders hanging, and I watch his instincts plume across his face as he ignores every one of them, and every night he leaves only when darkness has chanted itself onto the earth.

He develops a cough that I notice first, interrupting his conversations with the doctor to expel the wet air into his inner elbow, and he asks the doctor when I might be allowed to go home, and the doctor says they can't recommend release yet, and they don't want to create false hope.

The sunrises start to feel like failures and not-James tells me he's been going to the chapel and I want to beat my chest and refuse his prayers because the man I married would not believe that simply placing his body into such a structure could make a difference. Not-James tells me he feels less alone there, his ears cocked to the silent prayers of the hospital, and I tell him that I am his god, and I watch his chin start to twitch, but he doesn't deny it.

When he leaves, I let the starlight wash my eyes and watch as the world outside contracts into darkness, and I rub the lizard face of my elbow skin and listen to the old woman down the hall cackle and chuck anything within reach out the door of her room and hear a nurse drag a chair to set up camp until the woman is quiet and the nurse can loosen her clenched fists.

Hospitals, I realize, fill themselves full of accusations, of people believing certain truths about their blood and their hunger and their minds, and when another tries to force guidance on any of these topics, the impulse can be to travel as far away from these assumptions as possible.

Not-James's cough becomes a clay-packed wheeze unhitching itself from his lungs only to bind itself again and again. He talks the doctors into allergy tests. Mold comes back as a singular cause of his trouble, matching one of my many. They continue diving into the fungi spectrum and return with ergot as the answer, rye mold. I imagine the house furred with it now that we've been gone for days, a thin fuzz coating the walls and floor and furniture like on raspberries forgotten in the back of the refrigerator.

My body remains a slab in a loosening husk of skin and the sheets of my bed fill with black smears and the nurses want to know where they come from. I remind them of the mold that stuffs me, too. I worry aloud to them that I could infect the whole hospital. It is difficult to convince or remind or inform anyone of anything in my state.

James tries to convince me away, telling me to focus on getting better so I can come home. "But to what filth?" I ask, and his eyes clank over me, plundering me and trying to fill those gaps at once, and I recognize that our awe has tattered, as we buck and shatter against the tedium.

81

I SEE THAT the doctors are trying to diagnose Julie with internal battery. They're convinced her systems are attacking her from the inside. I know that these same shy symptoms hide within me, too. I experience the guilt of being only slightly more or less. I walk through my faults with open eyes. I say, *Yes, yes, yes.* I feel electric with self-wisdom. I suffer the sticky bile of jealousy and the magnetic pull of avoidance at once. I become beautiful with admiration for the diagnosed. I ignore all the other clues. I have been delivered an answer that satisfies.

Still my mind says, *Show them. Make appear what you know is within you.*

They don't at first know what they've found in Julie. I insist they check me for the same unnamed disease. The doctor says I look fine. He says that if it were meant to happen to me, I'd already be farther down in this chain reaction. I'd be whipping around at the end. I shake my head no. There is a spectrum that mustn't be ignored.

"Uncountable diseases might conceal themselves deep inside each and every one of us. Let us be thankful when they are not summoned to the surface." He speaks as if he were calling me to worship. He gives me a leaden smile. I want to resist and test him. I have always preferred knowing to wondering, *When?*

Julie is not restrained anymore. I can see her mentally chewing through the implied straps, though. She weaves her teeth together. She clamps down. She clads herself with that same involuntary grin. This time it alleges violation. Priests come by to offer simple blessings. Children parade through with balloon strings tucked in palms.

She seems improved. She is no longer the same eerie confluence of reactions she appeared to be on the roof. I ask her if she feels ready to go home. I ask her if she feels drained of that spirit. "Nothing's worth a burst of emptiness," she replies.

I wander the main thoroughfares of the hospital. I think of the back passages we were allowed through when we arrived. I think of the hidden hallways used to transport patients behind the scenes. I watch orderlies pull supplies from closets and cabinets. I stride through the idea of a place that never empties itself of people. Before a nurse can leave, he or she must be replaced by another. Air huffs through the heating ducts. Blood tunnels through my veins. It all calls our home to mind.

I go to the chapel to formally concern myself for a while. I drop my shoulders. I knit my hands loosely in my lap. I feel like a fugitive. The right thing to do is to stay with her in that room.

Maybe, though, her recovery relies on me letting her be. Everyone keeps telling me to take care of myself. They inquire about my cough. They tell me to rest. I keep wondering when Julie will feel that her whole mind has returned. I wonder if she ever felt it was gone.

82

THE DETECTIVES COME to the hospital, lending credence to the idea that even grave bouts of ill health can't save me from a bit of trouble. While James is off drifting through the halls and channeling the petitions of the other patients and visitors, I hear O'Neill and Poremski asking the nurse if it's all right to ask a few questions, and the nurse wishes them luck getting any sense out of me, and I snort, and the detectives appear, their eyes landing on me and taking off, trying to navigate their impressions of my reliability.

"Mrs. Khoury. How are you feeling?"

I chuff again.

"We hear you've had a rough go of it. Is your husband here? We'd like to talk to him, too."

I signal.

"Okay, if we give you some information, can you share it with him?"

I nod as if it were the most obvious answer in the world, but behind the gesture, I feel a skip of worry that the forgetfulness will swallow what they tell me.

"Mrs. Khoury, we had both the drawings in Ms. Abbatacola's home and the drawings at your house analyzed. Now, they match, but we also had them compared to the handwriting of you and your husband, and Connie, too, and there's no match there."

I hum. "So you believe us now that you have some harebrained version of proof? I'll go ahead and walk further out on this limb and say, it doesn't inspire much confidence when someone tells you they trust you because they've gone to great measure to prove they can. I'm not terribly accustomed to being doubted."

"We certainly don't mean to insult you, Mrs. Khoury. We haven't ruled anything out. We're trying to determine which avenues are worthy of our pursuit."

"Even better. Tell me, have you found our neighbor?"

"We have not."

"I could say I knew that would be the case but then you'd ask me how it was I knew."

"And by that you mean?"

"You, sir, are the detective. How long do we wait for Rolf to return? What happens with his property? His belongings?"

"Don't worry yourself about that. We'll look for him until he's found."

I start to smile, seeing through their platitudes, knowing a grin will be read wrong, but I can't call up the will to squelch it.

The detective eyes my wrong face. "Mrs. Khoury, I will remind you that any additional information you can give to us will be of the utmost help. We will uncover all of the relevant details, but you can help the timeline on which we do so by being forthcoming. That said, I understand you are currently in a fragile state, and I wish you a quick and uncomplicated recovery. Please let your husband know we visited and to contact us if he'd like to discuss the present situation."

"I'll do just that." I intend nothing, ring for the nurse.

83

"THE DETECTIVES came by," Julie tells me. I want to know more. She stays quiet.

The doctor visits. He says words. My hearing drops out over and over. I lose myself to the making of sense. "Temporal lobe epilepsy . . . Lying dormant for months, possibly years . . . During an attack . . . *Jamais vu* . . . 'Never seen' instead of 'already seen' . . . As if everything is strange, even home and family . . . Voices, music, people, smells, tastes called auras or warnings . . . Fright. Intellectual fascination. Artistic impulses. Delusions of grandeur and heightened religiosity. Even pleasure . . . You may think you're speaking, but you're not. You may think you're silent, but you're babbling . . . The temporal lobes—on each side of the brain at about the level of the ears where the seizure is focused . . . Some follow head injury or infection . . . Repetitive, automatic movements, like lip smacking and rubbing hands together . . . Spread to other portions of the brain . . . A convulsive, or grand mal, seizure . . . Completely or at least mostly controlled with medication . . . Candidate for surgery."

I can feel Julie's resistance without looking at her. Her refusal petrifies. I am grateful to have an answer that can explain her behavior. Her face, though, is pitted, stained with the shame of this defect.

"It's certainly not easy to hear, but better to have an answer, right, Jules?"

She stays still. More doctors come into the room, young and curious. They bustle to introduce themselves. I take each of their hands. I try to commit their names to memory. I stare at the stitched cursive on their white jackets. Julie refuses to accept their introductions. The doctors flounder and regain their bearings.

"I have a question, Doctors," she says. "Can you tell me where my bruises come from? . . . No, you can't, because everything is more complicated than you're making it out to be. If giving it a single name is some sort of comfort, well, lucky you, but I know there must be more. Go on, explain it all to me, since you have such a handle on the situation. Where does the mildew in our house come from? That's the result of my brain shaking itself apart? And the passages that open up in our home? Go ahead. You reason it all out. I'm listening. Sure, I'll sign off on a surgery. I'll corrupt some document with my name so you can cauterize the tiny coils of my brain, if *you* can solve the mystery of more than just me jumping off a roof."

The doctor listens. He looks at me. I can tell that he's certain this is all in her head.

I want to believe it is, too. "Julie, maybe you should rest. This is a lot to take in. We can make a decision tomorrow." I believe that treating her could be a start for us, a place to begin to heal and reorient ourselves, to zero in on why all of this began happening in the first place.

My tongue huddles silent in my mouth. The doctors say, "We'll check in with you tomorrow then. Good night." The light swings out of the room when they shut the door behind them. Julie and I fumble for ourselves alone in the dark.

84

MY BRAIN IS a flaking diamond, signifying rupture and un-ease. That is what I'm led to believe.

During the operation, two surgeons will take opposite ends of a coping saw and cut on the diagonal. They'll isolate the temporal lobe, the temporoparietal, the temporoccipital, the amygdala: the icon of my behavior, approximately invisible in the company of the other brains. They will ride one horse on the carousel of their attention, and they will look only when they are passing at the correct point, but lacking nerve endings, a brain cannot feel. These doctors will worm their way through my memories, trespassers, passing through, agog at what should have been fatal decades, like rooms in an abandoned house. At any moment my circuits could wake up and engage, form the intrinsic ties they have always tied, push back and reciprocate. The building of my body could come alive. Each expert will touch pieces they don't understand and classical time will lose meaning, as they spend almost a day pushing around up there, finally burning out.

I feel the need to trust their opinions, so that I can let someone else take control and try to fix things, but I cannot stifle the belief that it is me who best appreciates how my mind works, and it is me who best comprehends what I can live with and without.

In the morning, I tell them I refuse the surgery, and the doctors advise against this, saying my medicine has worn off, that the nosedive of chemicals has forced me into this decision. They tell me to wait an hour and see if I feel differently. But when should one make such a choice? On the drug-addled invention of a brain, or the scrambled twitch of a seizure? An ambulatory audience of physicians tells me who I am. After each of their efforts to convince me, I refrain.

85

ON THE EIGHTH DAY, Julie wakes up. I see her again, behind her eyes. Confusion and worry accompany her, but she is there. She is more exhausted on this day than the ones preceding it. It's as if, in waking, she's finally able to rest. I leave her alone. I go back home to see how it feels without her there.

I call Connie. I tell her Julie will be released. The surgery has been canceled. Connie pauses, as uncertain as I am that any choice could be correct.

I go online and research temporal lobe epilepsy. I learn that it's possible all brains have scarring. I learn that the damage might never express itself. People live their whole lives without knowing it's there. Temporal lobe epilepsy is a new diagnosis. The symptoms historically prompted the identification of any number of other disorders. I read about scientists claiming that Poe, Carroll, Van Gogh, Dostoyevsky, Kierkegaard—all of them—are thought to have suffered from the same brand of dysfunction. The evidence pointing to these classifications have been culled from their writing and artwork. The diagnoses form in hindsight, with only imagination as substantiation. The whole thing feels less like a mystery unraveled and more like a story being made up as it goes along.

I look up the allergen my body is reacting against: rye fungus, ergot. Formed on grasses and cereal grains, it lies dormant until spring or heavy rain create the proper conditions to trigger its fruiting phase. Ergot alkaloids cause a wide range of effects: restricting circulation and misdirecting neurotransmitters. Ergotism as another name for what is suffered when the mold has been ingested. A burning sensation that shows up in the limbs, the result of the constriction of blood vessels. Hallucinations and convulsions, nausea and loss of consciousness. Ergot extract is used to treat migraines and induce contractions and control bleeding and Parkinson's until hearts start to leak. The span between hurt and help is not a span at all: a fine dotted line. With no way to be sure, people bind all sorts of frenzy to ergot. Saint Anthony's fire in the Middle Ages, the Great Fear in the French Revolution, the hysteria of the Salem witch trials: everyone always looking for a solid answer.

I shut my laptop, and when my mind quiets with this new information, I hear the hum again, that chanting monotone that has no answer.

One can only identify something known; the unknown goes unseen. For every person diagnosed correctly, ten must be waiting for doctors to look past the possibilities they're already aware of. For every symptom on a patient's list, there are five that haven't been noticed and five gimmicks. For every ten times you think you see a person for who they are, there is one instance in which you correct yourself and realize she is so much more. What other disorders and conditions and diseases might look like what we've gone through? Medicine and rest seem unreliable solutions now.

I am tired, though. For now, I decide I must stick with the answers that have been handed to me. I stop looking for more.

I head to the basement with my camera. I set up my tripod in front of the hole in the wall where I knocked out the stain. The mold still clings to the edges of the plaster. This home comprises a collection of openings. Each provides access to our lives. Terrifying clues propose who we are and what consumes us.

I want to ignore these items and move on. I want to point at Julie as the problem and forget all the other evidence. I want to forget that I tore our home in half and couldn't stare at a work of art while remaining conscious. I want to blur this underscore of knowledge. I want my wisdom to attain a terrible flexibility. I want Julie to see how I've changed my mind. Incisive focus is no match for the dumb relief of a powerful resolution.

To be absolved of someone else's sin while still wondering what evil lurks within you. To name fate with nouns instead of adjectives.

I take more photos. I say, "This is only one way it might be," thinking of all the other ways. I'm either telling a lie or there are so many truths.

86

I RETURN HOME, still a bit loosened and unsteady, and the windows show the same warp, the light catching in the glass in different ways, the sunbeams circling, like a flashlight shifting and doubting softly, looking for proof. I can feel the pinching chill sneak around the frame, and then James opens his crooked mouth and asks me if a tooth of his is broken, and there's not enough light to see, but I lie, "You should get it checked out." He is buzzing hot, angry at the inconvenience, but I tell him not to worry, to rest and deal with it tomorrow, to forget action for now. I am happy to give him counsel, to feel that my opinion still counts. We live in the attempt to calm down for a moment, and I try to remember how to be near something without being worried by it and feel James's eyes on me, wondering if he can trust. I would do anything to release them. I make a nest for myself on the couch. James delivers me the stack of magazines and catalogs that arrived while I was in the hospital and lifts my feet into his lap. He flips on a baseball game and hits mute. Normal feels like a performance today, but we fake our way through, hopeful we'll grow into our actions.

On a commercial break, James says, "When you're feeling better, we'll sell the house." I agree, but we keep talking, even after the game returns on the screen. We doubt selling the house will provide answers to all of our questions, if any. I keep an eye on James, hopeful that I have defined the farthest end of this spectrum for us, but curious to discover if my mind is telling me the truth. I know now what it is to feel myself slip away, but what I don't know is how to move on with trust or how to be sure of what is solid. Like a pinball that moves backward with momentum as the bus it rides on moves forward, trying so hard to stay in one place. It is difficult to believe in any given trajectory, physics being an interpretation of the world and not an explanation.

I insist on making dinner the first night I am home. James has filled the refrigerator with guesses at what I'll want. All the raw materials stock themselves side by side, but I am unambitious. I make a lazy chicken curry, overspiced because of my resistance to dirtying measuring spoons. I pour in more coconut milk to counterbalance the spices and call it a soup. "Compared to hospital sandwiches, this is gourmet," he says. Yellow broth splatters his T-shirt as he slurps up a noodle.

I take myself for a walk. James offers to come with, but I ask to be trusted, only for an hour today. The grass has a bleached-out buzz, the summer sun having baked it dry. The forest is cooler, but the path is packed down and solid now. The wet spring leaves have dried and crushed themselves into dust. I

listen for the children in the trees and hear, *Cheer up! Cheer up!*
But then I see the robin singing the words. I search for proof
that the world is one way rather than another, but it doesn't
matter what is coming from inside us or around us. Our brains
allow it either way. We can lose ourselves behind a trapdoor,
whether in our mind or in the house.

87

JULIE'S PALE SHOULDERS are narrow, fraught with freckles. I have the urge to photograph each spot individually. It would never end. She sits on the edge of the mattress. The pillows sag naked. Her hands clutch the ball of dirty sheets in her lap. I should have remembered to wash them before she returned home. I never do. She turns her head to look at me. She still has the ability to stun me with her attention. I hear noise downstairs. I remember I turned on the radio when Connie paid us a visit earlier. I left it on so softly I could barely hear it, but in this room it fires full volume.

Julie's face is blue and friendly. She is sad and wants me to agree with her sadness. I look at her as if I know all of her angles. At one time I thought this was true. I remember us sitting on that couch in our apartment just months ago, perfectly cottoned. The white gold of availability around her irises strands her where she is. I know the tide will never pull me toward her. I am next to her, but away. She traces her eyes up to the ceiling when the tears form. I want to allow her to handle herself. I want to scoot toward her to welcome her to ask: for help, to be left alone, to be heard.

Julie chews the inside of her cheek. I can see it pulled in. I can see her jaw flex. A new habit? I pay attention. "I love you," I tell her.

"Even now?" That flimsy grin forms.

"Yes." We are many people. We separate. We tangle. We relock.

88

I NOTICE JAMES is wearing a loudly striped shirt he hasn't put on in years, one we argued about his keeping before the move. I realize he must have lost weight, and then I see it in his face, too. The scraggly strays of the top edge of his beard—the ones I wonder why he doesn't shave off—hide the new concavity of his cheeks. I wonder which worry has caused this. Did it start with the gambling or the house or when I went into the hospital? How long have I failed to notice him changing?

On the table, James has laid out the Realtors he's been researching. We agree we don't want to work with the man who sold us the house. James has put together a rough budget for improvements, researched home equity loans. He's been doing math, and from what I can see, his plan is sound: we could make money from a sale. I am touched by the effort this must have taken him, but I am still preoccupied with my own errors.

"I'm sick, but it's not just me. You can agree with that, right?"

"Of course," James says.

I dip my head, as if this were something I, too, am sure of, but I am uncomfortable with how all my lines of thought refuse to reconcile. If James is also sick, then no one here is well. I would prefer not to take all of the blame, but if we're both *not* sick, then something is haunting us, not only this place, but the woods, and the beach, and the house next door, and our memories and logic. There is still a chance that everything might be true, that we both might be filled with scars and substances that cause our synapses to fire inefficiently, that cause us to make decisions that are unwise and fantastic, and to believe what shouldn't be believed, but that is not to say that the world outside our minds is reasonable. That is just to say there is no sense in knowing where the line is drawn. We can mark the place that indicates *This is how much we can take*; we can monitor it, but that line, nevertheless, constantly moves.

89

JAMES AND I go to the neighbor's house and find the door locked, so we break a window. We fidget, but we get the job done. We find clues smirking everywhere: images of our home from decades before, family photos in what appears to be a time-line on the mantel, and we wonder how we missed them before: An engagement photo. Parents—baby. Parents—small boy—baby. Parents—two small boys. Parents—one boy. Parents—one boy—one baby. Parents—one boy—one girl. A father—two children. Two children as teens, alone. We read them like a story. We put together our version of the tale, the one we plan to spout confidently at grocery stores and bars. The family lost a boy and had a third child, but the girl was her own, could never replace the son who'd died. We realize that every story we heard in town might have truth, but we decide that just because this assumption we've formed about this story is our own doesn't make it any more legitimate or reliable than those we were told, and so we keep hunting.

We pinch oily pillows off the couch to sit on it and slide toward each other and realize the center springs have lost their strength. I stand to let James have his space as he flips through a binder to find news stories carefully arranged and yellowing in plastic protective sheets. He reads me the death notice for Alban Kinsler again, hoping something will have become clear since he tracked it down at the library. I pull stacks of velvet jewelry boxes off the bookshelves, but all of them are empty. James shows me a birth notice for Eleanor Kinsler, seven years the junior of Rolf, and I sit again. We page through prayer cards for names that don't match up with what we're looking for and newspaper articles marking the sorts of historical events that seem worth recording—centennials and local ribbon-cutting ceremonies—the stuff of small-town life. A death notice for Bette Kinsler, survived by husband Frederick, son Rolf, daughter Eleanor, reunited with son Alban. We find a real estate listing for the empty lot on which our home would be built. We find a prayer card made for Eleanor's funeral and perform the backward math of calculating her age to have been twenty-five at the time of her death. A newspaper story beside it shows a picture of the lake with the caption that the body of a young woman was found on the shore by a jogger.

Still it is not enough. We navigate the house easily, a mirror image of our own. I go to the kitchen, trying not to breathe in the rancid odor. Even the flimsiest of plastic containers are huddled together for reuse, all marred with a smear or speck of food unaddressed by scrubbing. I have the urge to stack them by size: yogurt cups into margarine tubs into gallon ice cream buckets, but I stop when I see the mouse droppings on the counter and then, when I realize what the tiny flecks are, I see them everywhere. I pull open the oven and then the dishwasher and the refrigerator, all unplugged, all filled with paper, mostly sheets folded into thirds: bills and statements and characterless summaries of the resources Rolf consumed in his life.

We climb the stairs to hunt for more. The master bedroom is perfectly arranged, but buried in dust, as if it hasn't been touched in decades. We open a wardrobe to find beautiful silk dresses and neckties, but no suggestions. James forages through a secretary desk, but uncovers only receipts. "A new car for only 580 dollars!" he exclaims, but moves on quickly.

I examine water damage on the wall near the ceiling and try to read a face into the spots. Slowly, I'm discovering the way my habits have conformed to the shape of the house.

A dresser drawer feels heavy even after I've pulled out the girdles and camisoles jamming it full. I convince myself of a false bottom and pry my nails around the inside edges and lift the thin sheet of veneer to discover cash and envelopes. I carefully lift the flap of the first, and the glue sticks a little. Inside, I find a letter addressed to Alban from "Mother." I ask James to retrieve the album of clippings from downstairs so we can compare dates, and he does. The letters are all posted after Alban's death. In them, Bette expresses her overwhelming grief. She praises Alban as her "Cupid child," perfectly beautiful, skilled, full of love. She writes, "I cannot bear to look at your brother. I know that your footing could not have faltered in that tree. How I wish the Lord had taken him instead of you." Other letters call out what must have been Eleanor's nervous locomotion, framing it as a sort of perfect energy around which they all revolved. "Her mind is so full of ideas. Her hands and lips always moving to write or say something that is already beyond my comprehension. She reminds me of you, my love, of what you would have become had Rolf not forced you from this life." Other letters show Bette's unraveling, admitting that it would be easiest if she joined Alban, that she can't force herself from bed most days so stuck is she in her dreams of this reunion, that she takes more and more of the pills prescribed by the doctor to calm her nerves and convince herself out of the house. "I dread the moment your brother's evil will resurface and take Eleanor from me, too. I have grown fearful of him. Your father disagrees, but he has always been blind to emotion, assuming the best in people and stepping away when something is too hard to deal with."

In another bedroom—one it is apparent has more recently been used—we hunt through shoeboxes. We find to-do lists broken into the addresses 891 and 895. Rolf's signature on documents for both. We find a framed photo on his bedside table of a young man and young woman. The young man looks directly at the camera, while the young lady, her hair rumpled, pulls away, staring off toward the woods behind her. If we didn't know better, we might have assumed it was Rolf and his young bride. We know, though, it must be Eleanor, anxious, even then, to hide.

James takes my hand, puckered and tarnished by the dirt that shakes off everything we touch. He recalls the children in the woods, shouting to each other, balanced in the trees, dropping. I mention the way the water at the beach threatened to pull us into it, that gentle sidestroke whistling us home. "The cave?" James asks. We don't have a hint about the cave, but we can create stories. We know enough now to see sense in it without understanding specifics.

James shifts and turns, looking for more, and I splinter into silent tears beside him. It is too much to know all of this now, after I accepted that it might have been contained within me. How do I return from that horizon?

"Read this." I hand him a journal, not unlike the one we found in our home, this one written in an adult hand, the script grown flawless.

> I pointed at a bottle of poison and asked my father what it was for. He refused an answer and hid it from me.
>
> Once again I found it and asked the maid. She took it from my hands and made it disappear.
>
> The last time I found it, I brought it to my mother. She accepted it as a suggestion and swallowed it down, losing herself in a slender jungle of pain and rupture. For the first time in ages, she held my eyes defiantly in her own and bade me to bear witness. "It is appropriate that you deliver me unto my death," she said. She believed this was my curse, one she could no longer bear: to push people to their ends.
>
> I should have called someone. I should have told her that that wasn't what I'd meant, but I could see, before the act was even complete, that everything would be easier from then on. Her resolve and fury evidenced themselves. I had given her the tool for an intention she'd been thumbing the edge of for a long while.
>
> Atropa belladonna. Atropa, from the name of the third Fate, Atropos, who cuts the thread of life. Bella donna: beautiful woman. Mother previously used the serum to dilate her pupils,

to make her eyes appear more seductive. Father used it to treat
his weak stomach. One substance, both to heal and poison.

Mother stayed close, twisting on her feather bed as a storm
ate away at the north-facing shore. Trees tipped into the lake.
Blissful digressions yarned from her mouth. Father joined
me in her room and we wound tightly around the moment. He
never asked why I didn't gather him sooner so we might have
helped her survive. Her face clouded with an ultimate doubt.
He held her hand as she gave way.

"It's not enough to believe we're haunted, though, is it?"
James asks.

I agree it is not. I refuse.

We give up, ready to return home, when we're jolted by the
pound of marching-band music from downstairs.

James looks at me, panicked. "Could he have come home?"
His thumb vibrates against the page of the book.

I'm so sure it's not that, I squeeze his shoulder. "I bet that
old turntable stopped spinning weeks ago and just kicked on
again." I lead the way down to the living room and pause at the
bottom of the stairs. I see a thick wool sleeve resting on the arm-
rest of the wing chair facing the fireplace.

"What?" James pushes past to pull the needle off the record
and I look away, hoping what I saw will be gone when I turn
back. "That's a good sign we should go, right? You ready?"

I cast my glance up the stairwell, then into the kitchen—
pretending to take it all in one last time—finally returning my
sight to the arm of the chair, and the fingers resting on the
handhold. James stands a few feet in front of it. If Rolf is sitting

there, there's no way James could miss him, but James's face shows only fatigue.

"I might make one more sweep of the place. Make sure everything is in order."

"Do you want me to stay?" James asks.

"No, you go ahead." I try, with all my might, to keep my eyes on James.

He kisses me on his way to the back door. "Don't stay long." He gives my hand a squeeze. He shuts the door behind him, and I hear a rasp, not unlike that breath that formed above us the night my parents stayed over. I walk toward the chair and see that the little finger of the hand is missing. I pause and push ahead.

I can't call seeing Rolf's face a surprise. We lock eyes, as we have so many times before through the windows, but this time I don't look away. I don't try to touch him. Neither answer would satisfy me.

I think hard about what I could possibly say. *Are you real? What happened? Do you need help? Have you done this to us?* No threats or statements shape themselves in my mind. I form only questions. I speak none of them.

He doesn't tell me to go. I don't stay.

90

ON THE BATHROOM mirror: a face drawn in lipstick. I wipe it off and don't mention it to Julie.

A plumber visits and can't find a reason for the mold.

A new bruise clenches Julie's ankle.

We bring in a contractor to give us an estimate on replacing the kitchen cabinets.

We look up tax credits for putting in new windows, ones that don't stretch the view outside into strange shapes and will keep the energy inside instead of allowing it to slip away.

My parents finally visit, for what will be the first and last time. My mother beams. My father's normally shadowy features gather up the light. They compliment every detail of the house. They wonder aloud why we would want to sell it.

"It's not for us," Julie says. "Something smaller, more manageable."

"This is a good house for children, though," my mother says.

Julie and I shrug. We avoid arguments. We invite them to sit down. We pour them water from distilled jugs we bought at the grocery store. The renovation excuses us from allowing them to stay here in the house with us. We say the water is turned off. We hope they don't test the faucet.

My mother looks out the window. "That old man next door will be sad to see you go. I'm sure he was glad to have someone to call on if he needed to."

I try to remember if we'd mentioned him to her or if we'd kept him a secret. I walk over to the window. I follow her gaze.

"Oh, there he goes," she says. She turns back to the living room. I cast a look at Julie. She shuts her eyes gently.

We don't comment on the noise that hums under our small talk.

We prepare ourselves to leave. We experience our fear privately. When I see an errant shadow, I tell myself it's nothing. When I notice a row of photos turned facedown on the shelf, I right them.

91

BACK AT WORK, my coworkers behave politely. They ask me how I'm feeling. I know they've been told I had an infection, but I note the questions in their eyes, wondering about details, trying to discern some other issue.

By the time I had recovered my senses, the flowers they'd sent to the hospital had died, but James saved every enclosure card. I wrote thank-you notes for these gestures and for the people kind enough to cover my work while I was out of the office. A prototype of the product I was spearheading has been fast-tracked, already moved into compliance review. Usually I'd be angry they'd gone on without me. I'd scour their specifications for miscalculations. This time, though, I commend people on pushing ahead.

I check my bank account online to see if a payment for a medical bill has cleared and see some withdrawals for small amounts from our shared account. James has not yet found a job. I tell myself the ATM visits are for incidentals and nothing more, until he can build up his own account again. I take my chances.

Connie treats me to lunch. "Beer? Wine?"

"I think I'll stick with water today," I say. "Sorry to disappoint."

"Very well, we'll be good. I'm ordering the cheese curds, though, for us to share."

I resolve to order the cheeseburger and fries, but when the waiter arrives, I chicken out and ask for a veggie burger and to sub a side salad. Connie squints and one-ups me, ordering a bowl of soup. She pulls up the batch of listings she's forwarded to me on her phone: town houses and single-family homes on the outskirts in new developments. She's glad James and I have decided to stay nearby once the house sells. I tell her I can't even think about buying a new place until this one is off the market, though. If it means we'll need to rent for a while, so be it. "Maybe renting is the way to go no matter what," I say. "A nice one-bedroom where we can see the whole place at once if we stand in the middle of it."

"Apartments mean more neighbors to deal with," Connie says.

"Ah, but they can't peek in if they're in the same building. They could see us come and go, and that's about it."

The summer sun is shining brightly through the window, and Connie mocks me when I put my sunglasses on inside. "Have the detectives been by to see you lately?"

I shake my head, tolerant of their absence. I feel that pang that's grown familiar—guilt at not mentioning what I saw in the house after James left. I consider telling Connie what James's mother spotted in Rolf's window, but I don't trust her eyes more than my own. "You?"

"Nope, but no further trouble. Repainted that wall and that seemed to be the end of it."

I search Connie's face for accusation, but she hides it well if it exists at all. Her trust has allowed her to move on.

"That has got to be the fifth double-wide stroller that's gone by today," I say, catching sight of another mother maneuvering down the street, willing to distract myself.

"Lots more twins these days what with fertility treatments. Soon everyone will be born with a double." Connie flares her eyes, risking spookiness.

I laugh, but I think of all the times I was alone, but didn't feel that I was, and vice versa.

92

A COUPLE COMES to look at our house. We tell them what improvements are in process. We uncover the secret passages one by one and watch their wonder unfold. They ask us why we want to sell it so soon after purchase. "It's too big for us," Julie says. "I had some health troubles and we want something more manageable."

I feel a spike of unease not telling them all of the other truths. They put in an offer right then for more than we asked. There will be weeks of busy work to be sure of the outcome. When we see the number they've written down on the slip of paper, though, we allow ourselves to feel relief. We walk them out. We tell them we'll be in touch. We wave them off.

I stare into the grip of the front door. I am ready to turn my back on this afternoon. Julie takes my hand, though. We sit on the porch swing. The air is still. We don't rock ourselves. We stay where we are.

We hear fireworks near the lake. It's not dark yet. We search the sky for the explosions. We can't find the light against light. The brilliance is lost without contrast. We hear the booms over the buzz of the interior.

We watch as those kids climb down from their trees and peek into the neighbor's house. Maybe we feel responsible because we broke that first window. It showed them no one was watching. It let them know advantages could be taken. Maybe we watch those kids pull out cans of spray paint and leave words behind. Maybe they hurl rocks. Maybe they turn the hose on. Maybe they light fires and scale the outside of the house like a mountain. We wonder what the kids call this game. Is it a game? We consider phoning the detectives.

"Let's not," Julie says.

"And when they ask us if we saw anything?"

"We haven't seen a thing."

ACKNOWLEDGMENTS

Unlimited rounds of gratitude dedicated:

To Claudia Ballard for her committed smarts and warmth and encouragement for the past four years.

To Emily Bell for believing in this book and taking it on, and for the amazing space she's made for bold women's voices. To the entire FSG team, especially Maya Binyam, for making this process even more rewarding than expected.

To Lindsay Hunter and Aaron Burch for delivering enthusiasm when I was at a moment of crisis and for being bold enough to serve tough advice. To Eileen Myles and Bonnie Jo Campbell for their astute guidance.

To the Vermont Studio Center and the Hald Hovedgaard Danish Author-and-Translator Center for the time and space to work on this project. My thanks and hope also go to the Illinois Arts Council. I am optimistic that Illinois will recognize, again, the importance of fostering the arts.

To Pam Harcourt, Andrew Cha, and Jon Evans, for the only writing group I've ever been a part of, short-lived as it was. This was born there.

To Zach Dodson for serving as a role model and for being a cheerleader all the way.

To Amelia Gray for her friendship and generosity and having my back again and again.

To the good people at Dzanc for everything up to this point.

To Lauren Spohrer at *Two Serious Ladies* and Ryan Bradford at *Black Candies* for publishing portions of this manuscript.

To Roger Ballen for his images, which pushed this book further.

To the long list of teachers who are with me every time I write.

To my employers for supporting this work.

To my family for understanding and believing in me before anyone else did.

To my friends for their kindness and distraction.

To Jared for everything else.